I0716927

ORACLE

COVEN: BOOK 7

DAVID NETH

DN Publishing

Oracle
Coven, Book 7
Copyright © 2022 by David Neth
Batavia, NY

www.DavidNethBooks.com

ISBN: 978-1-945336-24-9
First Edition

Subscribe to the author's newsletter for updates and exclusive content:
DavidNethBooks.com/Newsletter

Follow the author at:
www.facebook.com/DavidNethBooks

Also by David Neth

<u>Coven</u>
Harpy
Siren
Valkyrie
Shapeshifter
Sorcerer
Witch (Short Story)
Enchantress
Oracle
Trickster
Poltergeist

<u>Under the Moon</u>
The Full Moon
The Harvest Moon
The Blood Moon
The Crescent Moon
The Blue Moon

The Art of Magic

<u>Fuse</u>
Origin
Omertá
Oblivion

<u>Heat</u>
Black Magnet
Dust Storm
The Gatekeeper

<u>Standalone</u>
All I Ever Wanted

CHAPTER 1

- MAY 1983 -

The gardens were beautifully laid out in between the old mansions. It was such a wide lot that Oren wondered if there had once been a house standing where the gardens now lay or if the original builder of the mansion had always intended this lot to be used for nature's beauty.

Not that Oren was here to admire the flora. He had a much sinister intention.

It was the traditional end-of-the-semester celebration that the head of the history department threw for his students. As fun and generous as it appeared on the outside, it was also obvious that the professor certainly liked to be praised for his material possessions—whatever powered his ego.

Oren walked up the brick pathway from the sidewalk and

through the iron gate into the garden. The beauty of the yard was hidden behind large bushes. The professor wanted people to admire his property, but only when he invited them and only when he could hear their praises.

College students milled about, drinking cocktails, even though most of them probably weren't even old enough. Their chatter revolved around finals, moving out of the dorms, and summer plans. Few of them discussed career prospects greater than summer employment at Mike's Mini Mart and Gas Station.

The gardens were symmetrically squared off, with brick pathways framing four prominent flower gardens. Beyond, there was a small open grassy area beneath a large mature oak tree with a pergola that matched the same colors as the ornate brick house.

Oren made his way back to the pergola, where the drinks table was set up. He fixed himself a martini as he listened to the conversations behind him. It was imperative to find where the professor was before the professor found him.

Sipping the smallest of sips so as to keep a level head, Oren stood casually in the shade with one hand in his pocket and the other clutching his drink. He surveyed the yard and saw cliques of people grouped together in conversation.

Nobody appeared to be in the house at first. And then, Oren watched as a particularly inebriated young man nearly tripped down the brick steps when he exited the sunroom in his pursuit back to the drinks table. Oren saw a face in the porcelain throne in the young man's future.

Still, the access to the sunroom gave him an idea. Surely, it wasn't enough for the professor to idly accept praise for his house. No, he would want to encourage it by offering tours to students who would do any amount of sucking up to get a better grade on their final assignments.

Setting his drink on the table, Oren walked with purpose to the sunroom, anticipating questioning looks that never came.

Inside, the professor was finishing up a tour with a small group of students. He laughed and thanked the group for their comments and looks of wonder. Despite the casual nature of the party, the professor wore dark blue dress pants and a white button-down shirt. Most prominent of all was the red amulet that hung around his neck. It caught the light coming in from the windows in the sunroom and cast the space with bright red light.

"Thank you, thank you," he said, adjusting his perfectly-rolled sleeves on his biceps. "Yes, I am quite proud of my home. I'm certainly glad that you enjoy it as well." He noticed Oren and the smile deflated just a smidgen. Turning back to his students, he cranked up the strength of his smile and said, "Why don't you all go out and enjoy the gardens and, if you're old enough, a beverage?"

The group moved toward the door, ignoring Oren. The professor held the door open for them, then closed it behind them. With a flick, he locked it.

"I was wondering when I would see you again," he said with his back to Oren.

"You certainly didn't think that I wouldn't come for what is mine."

The professor turned and smiled at Oren. "What is yours? I acquired the amulet fairly."

"It was theft."

In his breast pocket, the professor reached for a pipe. "Mind if I have a smoke? I have a feeling that this will be a stressful conversation, although I'm confident that we can come to an agreement."

Oren motioned for him to continue, then looked around the room. "You know, I've been looking into you since you first entered my life. I'm intrigued by the fact that you've worked your way into high society."

"High society?" the professor asked, taking a puff of his pipe.

"You teach history at Gannon University. You have a stately address and a beautifully restored home. You have people fanning all over you."

The professor smiled, playing at bashfulness. "Well, yes, in that way I suppose you can say I am part of high society."

"You crave power of all kinds," Oren went on. "Academically, financially, socially…magically."

At that, the professor's head snapped up to Oren. "You think you're clever, don't you?"

"Not clever. Truthful."

"And what, may I ask, is your version of the truth?"

"My version is the only truth: you stole my family's amulet in your thirst for power."

"You see, that's not—"

"I want it back." It was painful enough to Oren for having lost it. But seeing it around another man's neck—someone who had no right to wear it—infuriated Oren.

"I'm afraid that is simply not going to happen." The professor pulled the pipe from his teeth and waved it at Oren. A streak of lightning shot from the end of the pipe and struck the plaster beneath the staircase behind Oren.

"I do not want to harm you, but you leave me no choice," the professor said.

"You've never hesitated to harm anyone before." Oren threw a small vial at the base of the professor's feet, which sent up a cloud of smoke in his face, making him cough. Oren raced forward, but was intercepted with a force so strong that it lifted him upward and across the large entry room.

The professor stepped out of the magical smoke and toward Oren, who scrambled back to his feet. The professor grabbed the front of Oren's shirt and forced him to his feet, pushing him against the wall.

"And to think, I didn't even need to use your family's amulet," he said. "That would be the just desserts you deserve, wouldn't it?"

ORACLE

The latch on the sunroom door jangled and a student knocked on the glass. The professor turned toward the noise. Oren didn't waste any time. He pulled the knife from his belt and drove it straight through the heart of the professor.

Immediately, Oren was drenched in the professor's blood. The clutch on his shirt loosened as the professor fell to the floor. The student behind the glass screamed as she watched the attack.

Oren needed to act quickly.

Snatching the amulet from around the professor's neck, he bolted to the front door and out onto the street. He ran without looking back. Even though the sorcerer had pushed him to murder—something he swore he would never do—it felt right. At the very least, he got justice for his family's loss.

CHAPTER 2

‑ FEBRUARY 1989 ‑

Samantha stepped out of the clinic into the gloomy, cold weather. She pulled her coat around her tighter and beelined for her car.

As much as she tried to downplay Steven's concerns about her health—she hoped that he would forget it altogether—she knew he wouldn't. And he hadn't so far. Which, she ultimately knew, was a good thing to have a husband care about you so much that they insist you go to the doctor when things are wrong. But it was annoying at times.

Samantha would rather not have taken the afternoon off simply to get blood work done, several days before her actual doctor appointment. She had the time, but it was still her first year. And in her industry, they were well into their busy season: tax season.

Samantha blasted the heat once she got to her car and glanced at the time. It was just after two. Too late to go back to work, but if she went home she'd feel guilty about being home, feeling as though she should be working instead. A bad mindset to have, she knew, but it was how she felt. She was a workaholic.

As she navigated her car out of the parking lot and onto Liberty Street, she decided at the last minute to turn right instead of left, swerving into the opposite lane, where an oncoming car down the street got nervous and beeped at her. She managed to swing back into her lane long before the other car passed.

Worry wart.

When she pulled up to the stop light at West 32nd Street, reality set in. That wasn't a safe thing to do and wasn't like her. Maybe there *was* something wrong with her.

In truth, she had only felt marginally better since she'd promised Steven to go see the doctor last week on Valentine's Day. Maybe getting checked out wasn't such a terrible thing. Still, she was worried about what the doctors might uncover.

Since she'd feel guilty going home, Samantha reasoned that she'd feel more accomplished with her time off if she was running errands. She turned left onto West 26th Street, drove several blocks down the overbuilt street, then sat in the shared turning lane waiting for traffic to pass so she could pull into the parking lot of the Apothecary.

It was an herbal shop she had discovered a couple weeks ago—one where she had certainly left an impression. One that she wanted to help clear up by frequenting it.

When she walked in, the woman behind the counter smiled at her as she recognized her.

"Welcome back," she said with a bright smile and a wave.

Samantha nodded. "Hello Margaret. How are you?"

"Not too bad." She came over from the cart of herb plants by the window with a watering can in her hand. "What can I do for you?"

"Actually, I came in to stock up on some herbs. I have a list here. Would you mind checking?" Samantha handed her a slip of paper from her grocery notepad.

Margaret set the watering can down on the floor. "No problem at all. I'll be right back." She stepped to the far wall and Samantha busied herself by looking through the rest of the items in the shop.

The Apothecary was different than Mystic Treasures, the other occult shop that she and Kathy usually frequented in Erie. The Apothecary had authentic magical instruments and ingredients, but they were limited. The stock was overpowered by novelty gimmicks like spirit stones and scented candles and wind chimes that alluded to the otherworldly, but didn't explicitly embrace it. Still, the shop offered enough of the basics that it wasn't a wasted trip.

"Hey Margaret," Samantha started.

"Hmm?" She tilted her head up toward Samantha, her focus still on the stock of herbs.

"You wouldn't happen to have any recommendations for, uh…fortune tellers or seers or oracles or someone like that, would you?"

Samantha had tried to consult with one several weeks ago before she really started to feel ill. But then several magical emergencies popped up, as well as the newlywed spats she'd been having with Steven, and finding the answer to the question that had been bothering her took a back seat.

The question got Margaret's attention. "Well, I don't know. You know, Laurie has a list of what she calls *specialists* in a notebook under the register, but I haven't looked too hard at it. I thought that it was quite silly, but I can check if you're interested."

"If you could."

"Absolutely." Margaret set the final jar of dried herbs in a basket along with the others she had collected and stepped back to the register. She pulled the book out and began to flip through. "Hmm…let's see here. Um…"

Samantha looked down at the book and did her best to read upside down. "Preferably someone who isn't just going to con me out of my money."

"Oh, of course," Margaret said with a fervent nod. She flipped through absently, clearly not really understanding the list.

Shamans, witch doctors, ghost hunters. From what

Samantha could read, the list was very much like the shop: authentic, yet disguised by gimmicks.

"Wait," Samantha called out suddenly. "What's that?" She put her finger down to the woman who had the title "oracle" listed beside her.

"Vanita Patel," Margaret read. "It says here she has a shop on Parade Street. On the corner of 11th."

"Perfect, do you mind jotting that down? You can just add it to the bottom of my list there."

Margaret transcribed the information, cashed Samantha out, and bid her farewell. Samantha stepped back out into the cold and looked down at the address. Was she desperate enough to see an oracle?

Then again, she had done crazier things in the last few weeks. She started the car and merged back into traffic.

Parade and 11th were across town, but Samantha didn't mind the drive. Fifteen minutes later, she pulled into a parking spot on the street in front of a row of houses that had been converted to commercial buildings a long time ago. They had seen better days.

The whole area, in fact, had the feel of vacant prosperity. Empty buildings, vacant lots of businesses torn down for crumbling parking lots. It wasn't the best image of Erie and it made Samantha nervous of what she was going to walk into. But it was the middle of the day and there was no one outside. Maybe this Vanita lady wasn't even open.

Oracle

Samantha stepped through the door of the small storefront on the first floor of the converted house. Inside, there was no remnant of a residential dwelling.

Red velvet curtains hung on the walls. Purple and gold patterned fabric hung from pins on the ceiling, sectioning off the sad looking waiting area from whatever lay in the back. The room smelled of incense and mildew. The whole atmosphere summoned up an image of this Vanita woman in Samantha's mind and it wasn't someone she wanted to meet for real.

Samantha turned and had her hand on the door in an attempt to escape when she heard someone behind her say, "Oh, hello. Are you here for a reading?"

No way to retreat now.

Turning, Samantha smiled. "Yes, sorry. I wasn't sure you were open."

"Nonsense, I'm here. I'm open. Come on back."

Vanita wasn't as bad as Samantha had imagined. For one, she had all her teeth, it seemed. She had her curly dark hair tucked up on her head with a series of bright colored headbands. Despite the damp chill in the room, she wore a T-shirt and a flowing skirt that matched the fabric holding her hair.

Samantha followed Vanita behind the curtain, where a wooden table sat in the center of the room. To the left was clearly the oracle's chair, as it was surrounded by boxes of trinkets, as well as magazines and newspapers and bottles of water. The other chair was a standard office chair.

"Have a seat."

Samantha set her purse on her lap and sat on the edge of the chair. She unwound her scarf, pulled off her gloves, and extended her hand. "I'm Samantha—"

Vanita threw up her hands. "Don't tell me! And don't touch me!" She laughed. "I know I sound—and probably *look*—crazy, but I try to start everyone's reading with a clean slate."

Samantha smiled politely. "Okay."

She narrowed her eyes and studied Samantha. "Hmm...you're obviously very independent, judging by the way you carry yourself and the fact that you're here alone. I don't think you're an only child, but I do suspect you're the oldest of your siblings. I'm sensing a lot of responsibility on your part, which speaks to your independence, so that makes sense."

Samantha was impressed. These weren't generalities like some so-called fortune tellers sprouted. These were specific— and correct—key points about her as a person.

"You're young, but not inexperienced. I'm guessing that you've already had to work for a lot in your life, so there is a touch of pride. However, you still have some drive because there's a lot more you want to do. And I'm also assuming you hold high standards for yourself, so you don't just settle for good enough. How am I doing?"

Smiling, Samantha said, "That was amazing. Dead on. Are you…are you, um…*gifted*?" She didn't know how to ask the "magic" question in case Vanita had just gotten lucky—or simply cheated somehow.

The oracle laughed. "Yes, honey, I'm magical. As are you."

"Right." It felt awkward to admit that, but clearly Vanita already knew it as soon as Samantha had walked through the door. Was there something about her that said, "Witch"?

"So what can I do for you, dear?"

"Well…I just got married—"

"Congratulations!" Vanita beamed.

Samantha smiled again. "Thanks. Anyway, my husband brought up the question of kids, and with…what I do, I'm just not sure that's such a good idea."

Vanita tapped her chin with her finger. "I see. Well, let's get a reading set up then." She dug through the boxes beside her chair, pulling out candles, incense, altar cloths, mirrors, the whole nine yards.

"You don't need to know more?" Samantha watched as Vanita spread the altar cloth out and arranged the candles on the table. She got to her feet and positioned the mirror to reflect the dim sunlight coming from the front window.

"No, dear," she said as she worked. "The reading is for you. You will see what you need to see. I'm simply the channel for the message."

"Interesting. But don't you read fortunes too?"

Vanita bent over behind the table and pulled out a lighter. She flicked it several times, igniting the incense until it began to smoke. "I do that when the client is not sure what they want to see. As I've already determined, you are very driven. You know what you want. We won't have any issues here."

She set the incense on the floor and sat back down. Stretching her arms across the table, she motioned for Samantha to take her hands, which she did.

"Concentrate on the question you want answered," Vanita instructed. "Forget everything else. Try to relax. Take deep breaths."

Samantha tried, but the incense made it hard to fill her lungs with fresh air. And the reflection from the mirror shining in her face made it hard to concentrate. But she kept her eyes closed and her hands in Vanita's.

Foreign words spewed out of Vanita's mouth and she gripped Samantha's arms with surprising strength. Samantha resisted the temptation to open her eyes and see what was happening, but then she felt her mind escaping her. As if she were lifting out of her body.

In a flash, she was struck with a vision. A dark alley at night time. A man lay in blood-covered snow, clutching what looked to be a fatal wound in his side.

Just as quickly as it came, it was gone. Samantha pulled away from Vanita and gasped.

ORACLE

"Well, *that* was unexpected," Vanita said.

Samantha snatched up her purse, her gloves, her scarf, and started toward the door. "I'm sorry, but I have to go."

Why did this keep happening to her?

CHAPTER 3

Kathy raced to the register. She had clocked in *just* in time and needed to be on the sales floor immediately. She felt like she'd been running from one thing to the next all day.

"Girl, where's the fire?" Leslie folded some of the returns on the second register.

"My bus was running late and I could only walk so fast across the parking lot, because heaven forbid the mall salts the sidewalks." Kathy snapped her name tag on her shirt. Afterwards, she straightened everything and checked to make sure the buttons lined up correctly. The store required her to wear the latest fashions to advertise to the customers, and her outfit—a nice blouse and black pants—seemed a little too formal for class this morning.

"Haven't you saved up enough for a car?"

"A car, maybe. Insurance and gas? Not a chance. I'm tapped out as it is and the last thing I need is another thing in my life." Once she was satisfied with her outfit, she let out a heavy breath and looked around. "Okay, what are we doing?"

Leslie indicated a basket full of boxes of heart-shaped chocolates. The rejects from Valentine's Day. "Ronnie wants us to mark those down to half price. They each need to be stickered."

Kathy nodded and reached for the sticker gun. Grabbing a box of chocolates from the basket, she checked the price and then adjusted it on the gun. "I swear, Leslie, I'm going to lose my mind. How do people go to school full time for *four years*? And to work on top of it?" She shook her head. "I'll tell you one thing, I have a lot more respect for people like that. My sister worked her butt off to pay her way through. I couldn't do it."

"You kind of are, though," Leslie said. "And if you need a breather, I'd be happy to take a couple of your shifts. You know I could use the money."

"I know, but so could I."

"Not at the expense of your sanity."

Kathy smiled. "I guess that's true."

"Special delivery!" Ronnie called from across the store. She weaved her way through the racks of clothes holding a large bouquet of lilies. She set them on the register in front of Kathy. "Who's the admirer?"

"For me?" Kathy's eyes grew wide as she looked at the bouquet. They were beautiful. She had never gotten flowers like this before. And she didn't count the one dollar carnations they sold during lunch periods in high school.

"They were just dropped off by a courier," she said. "There's a card."

"I see you've scoped this out already," Leslie said with a laugh.

"You know it!"

Kathy reached for the card. It was from Jeremy, which made sense, but was still a surprise. He was never usually the romantic type. Then again, maybe he was making up for Valentine's Day. They had just officially gotten back together a week ago to the day.

Kathy,

I tried to find something as beautiful as you, but nothing comes close. Enjoy the lilies. I'm proud of everything you're doing.

- Jeremy

If she wasn't standing in the middle of the store with an audience of Leslie and Ronnie, she probably would've cried. Those simple words meant so much to her: *I'm proud of everything you're doing.* No matter how tired she had felt moments ago, she now felt like she could take on anything.

"That's sweet," Leslie said, reading over Kathy's shoulder.

She folded it quickly and slipped it back in the envelope.

"What does it say?" Ronnie asked.

"The usual sweetness," Leslie told her. "So are things going better the second time around?"

Kathy was still smiling at the flowers and it took her a moment to realize Leslie was asking her something.

"Huh? Oh, yeah, they are. It's still new. We've only been back together officially for a little while, but we're both different people now. It seems to be working."

"I'm glad," Leslie said.

Ronnie examined the flowers again. "A man who sends you treats at work sounds like a damn fine man to me. Hold on to him, honey."

Kathy laughed. "Would you mind putting these in the break room so they don't get ruined up here? I have to figure out how to get them home safely on the bus."

"I'll give you a ride home," Leslie said. "Don't worry about it."

"Thanks."

Kathy spent the next half hour labelling the discounted chocolates, then stacked them back in the basket and carried them to the display by the concourse door. Ronnie wanted them somewhere where people could see them and draw them in to the store for the deals.

As Kathy approached the opening to the concourse, she saw Steven sitting at a small table near the coffee kiosk in the middle of the concourse. She waved, but he didn't see her. A moment later, a blonde took the seat across from him and they both started talking. They exchanged smiles and both seemed relaxed. Familiar with each other.

Kathy busied herself with stacking the chocolates, keeping an eye on her brother-in-law and his mysterious friend. She didn't know who this woman was and she wondered if Samantha did. By time she finished with the display, Steven and the blonde had finished their coffee. Together, they walked down the concourse to the door, still awfully chummy with each other.

Kathy didn't like it one bit.

CHAPTER 4

- AUGUST 1983 -

Oren thought the crowd would be safer.

He sat at a cozy little cafe somewhere in midtown Manhattan, a cup of coffee resting on the table in front of him. The cafe was busy, with people in and out grabbing their morning cup of joe, despite the temperatures already pushing the upper 70s at only eight o'clock in the morning.

In the three months since he had reclaimed the amulet, he had successfully avoided its recapture. Of course, that came with a cost: his sense of safety.

No matter where he went, Oren was constantly looking over his shoulder. The more he traveled, the more he risked someone coming and taking the amulet from him again. And staying in one place didn't offer much more of a reprieve. Lurkers could find him and corner him if he didn't keep moving.

However he looked at it, he just couldn't win.

And yet, after three months he thought he had mostly gotten the hang of this hiding thing.

Until he watched his sister walk into the cafe.

She didn't seem to notice him at first, the way she fished for her wallet in her purse and got in line to order. In fact, she didn't look in his direction at all until she had her cup of coffee in her hand and took the seat across from him at the tiny little table toward the back.

"You've been hard to find," she said after a hesitant sip of the steaming cup.

"That was kind of the point." Oren resisted having anymore of his coffee. With the way his heart was racing, the last thing he needed was more caffeine. How did his sister find him? He had been so careful!

After he snagged the amulet in Erie, he stayed in the Catskill Mountains for a while. At the time, he had figured that he would be able to anticipate any attack in solitude.

But then he got in his own head and worried that he could be watched without even knowing if someone knew the land better than he did. And, being that he had spent his whole life in the city in a quiet, nice, safe neighborhood, *most* people probably knew how to survive in the wilderness better than he could.

So he came to the total opposite of solitude: New York City.

Here, he figured the crowds would keep him safe. If something were to happen to him, he could make noise and draw attention, which would give him enough opportunity to escape.

Only, now that he was face-to-face with the very person he had been running from, making noise was not something he was even tempted to do.

His sister sat back casually and crossed her legs. "What could I offer you for the amulet?"

"I don't know what you're talking about." He reached for the coffee and took a sip to try to hide his face.

"Oh, come on now, Oren," she said. "We both know that's a lie."

"Okay, you want to know what you could offer me?"

"That *is* the question I asked."

"Nothing."

"Certainly, we can come up with an equal trade, Oren. It's not as if you're giving it to a *stranger*."

"I may as well be."

"Don't be like that. Look, I'm sure you've had a hard time these past few months trying to keep it safe. You haven't gotten much sleep. You're likely paranoid of everyone around you. Wouldn't it be nice to have a little break from that?"

He didn't say anything. It *had* been a long couple months. Honestly, it had felt like years that he had been protecting the amulet. He didn't know how much longer he could go on like this.

"How about I take it off your hands for a couple months," she suggested. "Say, two months and then we meet at a location that only the two of us know about to make the exchange. Then you keep it safe for a couple more months before passing it back to me. This way, we can both claim what is ours while we each get a break from the constant fear and worry."

Oren thought about it. It would be nice to have a break. He daydreamed of being able to go wherever he pleased without also bringing a weapon. He thought about how he could go back home and actually begin grieving the loss of his parents.

But none of that changed the fact that he knew he couldn't trust his sister.

"No," he said firmly.

"You haven't even considered it!"

"There's nothing to consider."

"Oren, I think we can—"

"You need to leave. And leave me alone."

His sister studied him as she bit the side of her cheek. Finally, she said, "Well, I can sense that you don't have the amulet on you anyway." She stood. "But I promise you this, I will search for it. And I will find it."

CHAPTER 5

Samantha stepped into the mall feeling flush from her mad dash to find Kathy. That didn't deter her from power-walking to the clothing store that had employed her sister for nearly six months now. Surprisingly, it was one of the few times Samantha had come to visit her at work.

But this wasn't a social call.

Kathy stood outside the dressing room, refolding the clothes customers had rejected and left inside.

"I need to talk to you," Samantha said breathlessly.

Kathy jumped at the sudden appearance of her sister. "Holy hell, Sam! Don't sneak up on me like that." She let out a frustrated huff of air and turned back to folding a shirt. "What are you doing here?"

"It's a long story. Do you think you can go on break?"

The younger sister glanced at the time. "I was planning on going in a couple hours around dinnertime so I could eat. Besides, I just got here about an hour ago. Can't you just tell me now?"

Samantha sighed and looked around. It was certainly possible for her and Kathy to have a private conversation among the racks of clothes, but what if someone overheard them in the dressing room? Or someone started looking at clothes on the next rack and overheard them? How much detail could she give without telling bystanders that they were witches?

"Or can it wait?" Kathy asked at Samantha's hesitation.

With a shake of her head, Samantha said, "I don't think so." Still, she paused, debating on how to start. The image of the man in the alley replayed in her mind. It was so vivid and yet didn't offer much in the way of information.

Kathy set a folded shirt on a pile and started on the last article of clothing. "So? What are you waiting for?"

Samantha looked back at the dressing room and Kathy rolled her eyes.

"Sam, there's no one in there. The store is relatively quiet at this time of day. It won't pick up until later."

That was a good point and helped Samantha feel safer diving into her story. "Well, I got a vision."

"A vision?"

Samantha nodded.

"You don't get visions."

"Today I did. I think it was of the future."

Kathy cocked an eyebrow as she moved the last piece to the folded pile. She turned her attention to her sister and crossed her arms. "When does this vision take place?"

"At night sometime."

"That's…vague. What did you see?"

"A man, uh, murdered."

Kathy looked surprised. "Murdered how?"

"I'm not exactly sure. I just saw lots of blood."

"You're not giving me a lot to go on."

"I know, but there's never a lot to go on with these types of things," Samantha said. "But I need your help."

"I'm working! And aren't you supposed to be too?"

"I had to get blood work done."

"Oh yeah. How did that go?"

"It was fine. But you're changing the subject. We need to find this guy."

Kathy sighed again. "All right, look. You said the vision took place at night, right?"

Samantha nodded.

"It's hard for me to tell in this windowless prison, but I think it's a safe bet that it's *not* currently night time."

"Right, but—"

"So we have time to stop anything from happening to this guy," Kathy said.

"True, but there's only one problem: I don't know exactly *where* it happened."

"Are you kidding me?" Kathy exclaimed. She glanced over at the woman several racks over, then lowered her voice. "Do you even have any idea where it might have happened?"

"An alley?"

Kathy closed her eyes and took a deep breath. "So you're asking me to leave work early?"

Samantha shrugged. "Do you think you could?"

"I could ask, but I'd rather not lose the hours."

What's more important: a man's life or a few extra dollars in your pocket? Samantha thought to herself. But that wasn't fair. She knew how hard Kathy was working to establish herself and contribute to the household.

"It's fine," Samantha said. "I'll just go by myself and scout out locations. If I get a jump on it, I can figure out a game plan to stop the attack from happening." She began to turn away, but Kathy called out to her.

"Wait!"

Samantha looked back at her sister, who was pinching the bridge of her nose. Something that Samantha knew she was guilty of whenever she was trying to figure out a problem.

"You going by yourself is a bad idea," Kathy said. "Um…let me talk to Ronnie, my manager, and see if she can call someone in to take my shift. I might not be able to leave right away, but I can ask. I'll also have to call Jeremy too. We were supposed to have a date tonight when I got out."

"Don't you work until, like, nine o'clock at night?" Samantha asked. "Where could you go on a date that late and not feel rushed?"

Kathy smirked. "His apartment."

"Ah. I see."

Turning to head further into the store, Kathy called over her shoulder, "I'll ask and see what I can do."

CHAPTER 6

- AUGUST 1983 -

Oren raced back to the tiny studio apartment that he was subletting from a college student who was currently on summer break.

Inside, he wasted no time digging into the bag of items he had just bought from the cornerstone on his way home. It wasn't much, but it would supplement the divination essentials he had with him at the apartment.

No matter where he was, he tried to keep a wide variety of candles and trinkets that he might need in a reading or seance or spell. As his father used to say, "You never know when you might need them."

How right you were, Dad, he thought to himself. He missed his father terribly.

ORACLE

He pulled a chair in the corner of the studio and stood on it. He pushed up one of the acoustic tiles on the ceiling. Stashed on the top of a nearby ceiling tile sat his family's amulet. He had moved it to several different hiding places throughout the apartment already, never trusting one place for too long. This ritual that he was about to perform would, hopefully, bring an end to that paranoia.

From the grocery bag, he pulled out what he needed: a bottle of vinegar, dried monkshood flowers, flaxseed, and a container of crushed red pepper. Moving to his suitcase on the bed in the small studio, he retrieved a single purple candle. It was half melted, but it would still do the trick.

Each of the items served a purpose in the ritual he prepared. The purple candle represented strength, protection, and success. The vinegar aided with banishment and protection.

Most important of all were the last three items. Monkshood helped with invisibility, protection from evil, and helped redirect enemies from coming after you. Flaxseed, when mixed with red pepper, helped protect against hostile magic and also helped expel negative energy.

Oren worked quickly and efficiently in preparing the ritual, using the few random cookware dishes that the student had stocked in the tiny kitchenette. First, he crushed the dried monkshood flowers in a pot. In a separate container, he mixed the flaxseed and red pepper together, then added the combination to the pot with the monkshood flowers. After draining the bottle of vinegar over top of it all, he struck a match and lit the purple candle.

Sitting on the floor with his legs crossed, he held the amulet in his hands, called up his family's magic buried within the magical trinket, and recited:

Protect me from my enemies.
Hide me from those who seek.
Protect me from animosity.
Empower my words and let it be.

The amulet in his hands shined a bright red. The light washed over his body, then dissipated. He didn't feel any different, but he knew that the spell had taken effect.

Now hopefully it would work the way he intended it to.

CHAPTER 7

"What about *this* alley?" Kathy asked with a bitter tone. She was irritated, through and through. The lack of information, the cold, the walking, the late hour. All she wanted to do was go home—or better yet, spend time with Jeremy. Their relationship was off to a fresh start and he was really making an effort. She needed to return he favor. Plus, she resented how she was forced to lose hours and would therefore have a smaller paycheck because of it. Luckily, Leslie was willing to finish her shift.

Samantha stood at the end of the alley on 10th Street, beside the Erie Playhouse Theater. The end of the alley opened up to a parking lot. She made a face. "This doesn't look right either."

Kathy groaned. "We've been to every friggin' alleyway that

we could think of!"

"I told you it was near a brick wall!"

"These *are* brick walls!" Kathy gestured down the alley.

"Not *that* type of brick."

Kathy bit back her anger. The sleep she'd missed out since the semester started was eating away at her usual carefree attitude. "Why don't you give me a little more than, 'It's near a *brick wall!*'"

"I'll know it when I see it."

"And by that point, I'll have *completely* lost feeling in my toes." Kathy buried her hands deep in her pockets and tucked her chin beneath her scarf.

In the streetlights, the women could see their breath. Worse, their feet crunched in the snow and if anyone living in the northwest knew anything about winter it was this: the crunchier the snow, the colder the temperature. Each footstep served as another reminder that they were battling against nature in this endless pursuit.

"Let's see if there are any alleyways down this way," Samantha mused as she led them away from the Playhouse.

"Now you're just guessing?"

"Eliminating possibilities."

"So guessing," Kathy clarified. "Why don't you tell me how you even got the vision in the first place? Maybe that'll help us find where this supposed murder might've happened."

"Will happen," Samantha said. "And it's not just a

possibility. I definitely saw it."

"Whatever."

Samantha continued around the corner onto State Street, where several cars zipped down the street to beat the lights before they turned.

"So…are you going to tell me?" Kathy pushed.

"I got the vision when I…went to see an oracle."

"An *oracle*? You realize we can do some of that at home on our own, right?" What was odder was that Kathy didn't think that Samantha was the type of person to consult an oracle. She had a hard time trusting people and, despite being a witch, she was more likely to believe hard evidence and not speculation.

"I wanted to see someone who specializes in it."

"You needed a specialist for what, exactly? Did you just have a hunch that this guy was going to get murdered? Do you know him? Could we have been staked out in front of his house this whole time instead of wandering downtown aimlessly?"

"No, I don't know who he is."

"Then what's the deal with the oracle?"

"I had the afternoon off."

"Oh, sure. Whenever I have some free time, I *always* go see a psychic!"

"Not a psychic, an oracle."

"Whatever." Kathy bit her tongue on her next snarky remark, suddenly hearing the attitude she had. "Sorry. I'm just cold and tired and uncomfortable."

"It's fine."

"But seriously, why did you go talk to her? Was it about how sick you've been feeling?"

"Yeah, that's it."

Kathy wasn't buying it. Perhaps Samantha already had her own suspicions that Steven was stepping out on her. Maybe she was being vague to make up for the fact that her fresh marriage was crumbling? But Samantha had never kept secrets like that from Kathy before.

"You know what?" Samantha said. "I'm tired and we've been out here forever. We should get inside and warm up. We've done the best we can to find him tonight."

"Maybe tonight's just not the night."

"Or maybe tonight *is* the night and we just haven't found him yet," Samantha said. "Maybe he's already lying in the snow bleeding out somewhere."

Kathy stopped in her tracks. Neither of them would be able to live with the fact that they turned their backs on someone they could help. "Then what do you want to do, Sam?"

Samantha looked around, scoping out any other potential alleys. She let out a deep breath, which Kathy could see dissipate around her slowly. "Let's just go home. I'll talk to the oracle tomorrow and see if she can give me any other indication as to why I got the vision. Maybe it was meant for her instead and I just intercepted it."

"Are you sure that's what you want to do?"

Again, Samantha looked around and considered. "No, that's not what I want to do. But we've been out here for two hours already and haven't found him. Let's go back to the car."

As Kathy followed her sister back to the parking lot several blocks over, she knew Samantha was not going to let this go easily. Her sister was a problem solver. And if she saw an innocent man get hurt, she wasn't just going to ignore him.

Besides, as much as they tried to convince themselves otherwise out here in the cold, they both knew that Samantha had gotten that vision for a reason.

CHAPTER 8

You still can't get warm?" Jeremy came back into his room and shut the door behind him.

Kathy shivered under the three layers of blankets. Despite being back inside for an hour, she hadn't been able to get the chill out of her. Her toes and fingers were still ice cold, despite the heat cocoon she was slowly creating.

"I was outside for a couple hours," she said. "I think I have the right to still be chilly."

"So you never found the dog?"

That was the story Kathy had spun for why she needed to cancel—then reinstate—their date. She claimed that along her bus route she saw a stray dog and went back out to find it before night came and the temperature dropped further. She didn't like lying to him, but it was the only way.

"No. I hope someone else found it and took it in."

Jeremy pulled back the covers so he could slide in beside her. Kathy curled away from the open air.

"Aw, and I was just getting warm!" she groaned.

He sidled up next to her. "Relax, I thought I could help warm you up."

Wrapping his arms around her, she leaned into his embrace and the welcome warmth of his body heat.

"Much better," she said.

Jeremy kissed the back of her head. "So how was your day? We never really got a chance to talk."

"It was okay. Got more homework, not sure when I'm going to do it. Worked for a bit before I decided to find that dog. Oh, and when I was at the mall I saw something I'd rather not see."

"The remnants of fornication in the dressing room again?"

"Ew, no. I saw Steven…and he was with a blonde woman."

"So?"

"They looked pretty cozy, Jeremy."

"You think he's cheating?"

She sighed. "I don't know."

"Well, what exactly were they doing?"

"Having coffee. Smiling. Laughing. Then they left together."

"Oh my. Alert the church leaders! How dare a man and woman enjoy *coffee* together! And *smiling*? Burn her at the stake!"

Kathy pulled away to glare at him over her shoulder.

"I'm kidding," he said with a chuckle. He pulled her closer. "It just doesn't seem like anything to worry about."

"You didn't see it. There was definitely a vibe between them."

"Did you tell Samantha?"

"No!" Again, she pulled away to look at him. "Do you think I want to destroy my sister's marriage on a 'maybe'? I need proof before I say anything."

"You two have always been able to tell each other the truth," he said. "And you've always told each other everything—as annoying as that is for me sometimes."

She grinned. "At least you still get the approval."

"Gee, thanks. But seriously, Samantha will appreciate the honesty, even if that *audacious* act you witnessed turns out to be innocent."

Kathy rolled her eyes at the comment, but knew he was right. She should tell Samantha. Her sister was confident enough not to take her anger out on Kathy for delivering the message.

But the idea of potentially driving a wedge between the new marriage was not one that sat well with Kathy. She needed more proof.

"I take it you don't like that idea," Jeremy said in her silence.

"I'll think about it," she said. "Maybe tomorrow her and I can have a chat."

CHAPTER 9

I'm telling you, I got that vision for a reason." Samantha stood at her dresser and rubbed lotion on her face. She glanced in the mirror to make sure she didn't miss any.

Steven lay in bed, the covers pulled over him, and his eyes droopy. "Mm-hmm."

"So it just feels wrong for me to go to bed when that man is possibly getting murdered out there somewhere right now." She gathered her hair up and piled it on top of her head as she stepped to the closet to look for her outfit for the next morning. "I feel like I should be out there right now, but Kathy insisted that we come home."

"It's twenty degrees outside," Steven muttered. "She kind of had a point."

"Eighteen, actually," she corrected. "I heard the weather on the radio after I dropped Kathy off at Jeremy's." She reached for a sweater and hung it on the hook on the back of the bedroom door. "Which is even more to my point. Maybe we can save that man if we can get to him in time. But instead, if he's lying in the snow and bleeding out, there's no way he'd survive. From the cold or the knife wound."

Steven rolled onto his back and stretched with a yawn. "Are you sure you're not taking on too much by yourself again?"

"I told Kathy about it immediately and she was with me the whole time we were searching for him. *And* I even agreed to turn back when she complained it was too cold."

"But you haven't stopped thinking about it since."

Samantha grabbed a pair of black pants and added them to the hook with the sweater. Satisfied, she pulled her hair tie out and sat on the edge of the bed.

"I can't help thinking about it," she said. "If I'm responsible for this man dying—"

"He's not going to die," Steven said. "If what you said is true and you got that vision for a reason, then somehow you'll end up in his path. Until then, I don't want you obsessing about this and losing sleep. You have a lot on your plate as it is." He reached for her, but she ignored his touch and she climbed beneath the covers.

"I know I've made mistakes recently with biting off more than I can chew, but my track record up until that point has been pretty good," she said. "I've always been able to manage, until I didn't. And that still haunts me. But I don't want to be questioned every time something comes up."

Two weeks ago, she had tried to save a witch from joining a demonic coven. With the amount of stress that Kathy had been under with school and work, she didn't want to burden her with another problem so Samantha tried to help the witch herself. Unfortunately, it was a bigger job than she could handle on her own and the witch was killed by another demonic creature who didn't want that coven growing any stronger.

The death had left cracks in Samantha that would last with her forever. A reminder of her failure. One that she could never correct or make up for.

Steven sighed. "Come here."

Samantha kept her stony expression, but allowed him to take her hand. He kissed the back of it.

"I'm sorry. I wasn't trying to doubt you. I trust your instincts, but even you have to admit they've been a little off lately."

She shrugged her agreement.

"I just don't want you to get hurt. I want you to be careful."

"I will be," she promised.

"By the way, how did it go with the blood work today?"

She fluffed her pillows and sunk deeper beneath the covers. "It was fine. They did the whole vampire thing and sucked some of my blood out. Made sure I ate a snack afterward and drank more fluids the rest of the day. No biggie."

"And you have the doctor's appointment on Friday?"

She rested her head against the pillow and stared at the ceiling. "Yes."

"Do you want me to go with you?"

Looking over to meet his eyes, she said, "I'd rather go by myself. That way, I have a little time to process whatever news they tell me before I have to really talk about it with you or Kathy."

Steven's face drooped for a split second, before he pulled it into a tight grin and nodded. "That sounds like you. Okay, I'll stay back then. But I want to know as soon as you get home. Promise?" He held out his pinkie.

She smiled and hooked her pinkie in his. "Promise."

CHAPTER 10

- AUGUST 1983 -

Sitting on a bench in Grand Central Terminal, the sister closed her eyes and focused on what wasn't outwardly apparent: her third eye.

With her third eye, there were no barriers. Time, space, resistance—it all faded away. If she could bring herself to a state of true harmony, nothing would be off-limits for her to see— past, present, or future.

Trouble was, she was having a hard time *getting* to that harmonious place. The station was too damn noisy. Still, she could see more than most people could. She was an oracle, after all.

Not that that was helping her now. She had searched everywhere, sensed every emotion, basically scanned every corner of this damn city to locate Oren. She had come up empty every time.

How had Oren been able to completely disappear off the face of the earth in a matter of twenty minutes? That wasn't enough time for him to catch a train or a bus. And he certainly hadn't *walked* out of the city.

Magic was definitely involved. Worse, the amulet was likely involved as well. And no matter how much the sister concentrated; no matter how perfect the conditions were, she wouldn't be able to find him if he had used the amulet to conceal himself.

The sister snapped her eyes open and caught a man trying to snatch away her purse from where it sat on the floor by her feet.

His eyes grew wide as she stared him.

"Looking for something?" she asked.

He tried to back away, but she stood and followed him, picking up her pace as he started to run. After he was out of her sight, she slowed and let him leave. Chasing him and making him pay for his attempts at thievery would only momentarily sate the anger boiling in her.

She needed a new plan. She needed to find Oren, even if she couldn't rely on her magical abilities to do so. She needed a pawn.

CHAPTER 11

The wind cut through all of her layers as Kathy crossed the street from the bus stop to Steven's office. She stepped up to the glass-faced building and stepped into the lobby, grateful to be out of the wind. In her reflection on the glass, she fixed her hair, then pulled off her scarf and gloves.

Inside the lobby, Kathy perused the directory, searching for Steven's office. Erie Accounting Corporation was on the second floor in Suite 209. She searched for the stairs, but could only find the elevator. Grumbling about encouraging laziness, Kathy hit the call button and waited for the doors to open.

After a good night's rest and thinking more about what she'd seen in the mall, Kathy had decided against breaking her sister's heart and implanting mistrust in their marriage.

Instead, she wanted to approach Steven himself. Give him a chance to explain what was happening and come clean to Samantha on his own. It was Kathy's way of offering them an opportunity to strengthen their marriage instead of tainting it.

She had intended on talking to him when they both arrived home later, but after sitting and staring at her homework all morning she had conceded to the fact that she wouldn't be able to focus until after she had talked to him. The only thing running through her mind were different scenarios of how the conversation would go and how Samantha would take it once she knew.

The elevator doors opened and Kathy stepped on, hitting the button for the second floor. Less than a minute later, she stepped out into a quiet hallway and followed the directional signs for Suite 209.

It was located at the end of the hallway with a giant sign indicating Erie Accounting Corporation, distinguished with its green and gold logo. Both colors that related to money. How subtle.

Inside was an open office, divided only by cubicle walls arranged creatively to conceal everyone. Only the front receptionist was immediately visible after entering through the front door. Several chairs flanking her desk indicated a small waiting area.

"Can I help you?" the woman at the desk asked with a practiced smile. She was older, maybe in her fifties, but still with blonde hair that looked natural. It was coiled up tightly behind her head. Her glasses perched on her nose. The name card on her desk indicated her name was Trudy.

"Hi, I'm looking for Steven Harper." Kathy tried to speak quietly so as not to disturb anyone. In the maze of cubicles, she could hear murmured conversations. Somewhere near the back, someone was laughing. Faintly, she smelled a mix of coffee, printing paper, and cigarette smoke.

"Do you have an appointment?"

"No, I'm his, uh, sister-in-law." That was still weird for her to think about. Sure, Samantha and Steven had been together for four years now, but it was only recently that she had a title to give him when defining her own relationship with him.

"So this is a personal matter?"

"Well, I guess so. It'll just be five minutes." At least, Kathy hoped that was true. How long did it take to point out someone's indiscretions?

"Let me see if he's available." Trudy reached for the phone and dialed. She kept her eyes down on her desk as it rang. After a minute, she hung up and checked the extension sheet beside the phone. "Hmm…he must've stepped away from his desk. Let me try another line."

The second time didn't bring any better results.

"Is he not here?" Kathy asked.

"Let me try his supervisor. Perhaps he's in a meeting." Trudy dialed yet another extension, this time for someone who answered. "Oh hi, George. Is Steven Harper in a meeting with you?" Her eyes flicked up to Kathy, then back down. "Hmm, well his sister-in-law is here to speak with him. Yes, she says it's a personal matter that will only take a moment." She held the receiver and looked up at Kathy. "Is this an emergency?"

"What? Um…I guess not—is he not here?"

Trudy ignored the question and returned to her phone. "No, it's not an emergency.…Yes, I'll tell her. Okay. Thank you, George." She hung up the phone and looked up at Kathy. "Mr. Harper is not available right now."

"He's not here, is he?"

Out of the corner of her eye, Kathy saw a woman walking from the cubicle just to the right of the entry. She had a stack of papers in her hands, obviously returning from the copier.

"I'm sorry, ma'am, but I'm not certain where he is," Trudy said.

"Where who is?" the woman from the copier asked.

Trudy opened her mouth to respond, but Kathy blurted, "Steven Harper. I'm his sister-in-law."

"Oh, you just missed him," the woman said. "My desk is next to him and we chitchat from time-to-time. He said he was taking an early lunch with a colleague."

"Someone from here?" Kathy asked. "Like a work meeting?"

The woman shook her head. "I don't know. It didn't sound that way, though."

"Why do you say that?"

"Everyone here knows each other, so he wouldn't have said 'colleague.' And if he's going to meet someone about one of his cases, we usually call them a 'client.' My guess this is someone else. Do you think he's interviewing for another job?"

"Thank you, Bernie," Trudy said dismissively.

Kathy flashed a smile to disguise her concern. "Thank you both. I really appreciate it. I'll just have to catch him later."

"No problem," Bernie said with a smile.

After leaving the office, Kathy's mind raced with the possibilities of where Steven could've gone. None of them sounded good.

CHAPTER 12

"Samantha! Welcome back!" Vanita smiled brightly when she came out from behind the curtain at her shop. "Honestly, I'm a little surprised to see you back here after the way you ran out yesterday."

Samantha cringed. "Yeah. I'm sorry for that."

"Did I do something to spook you?"

She hesitated, then indicated the space behind the curtain. "Can we sit down?"

"Certainly." The oracle led the witch toward the back of the small shop, and they both took their seats. Once in her chair, Vanita stuffed candles back into boxes, folded up altar clothes, and rearranged the stacks of newspapers and magazines on the small table. "This place is a mess! Everywhere I turn, I'm bumping into something!"

Samantha ignored the comments, eager to get right to the point. She had a hard time focusing all day at work. Even though she had been swimming in reports and documents and receipts and files, her thoughts had been on the vision. Worse, time seemed to tick by slowly the more she watched it. So naturally, the first place she came after work was to Vanita's shop. She needed answers. She hoped she could save that man from her vision.

"During the reading yesterday, I experienced something…strange," Samantha started.

Vanita chuckled. "Strange is kind of what I do, honey. I'm sure you've dabbled in strange as well."

"True. But this was…different."

"This has been bothering you since we last saw each other." Vanita met Samantha's eyes and stared intensely.

"I guess it has."

Vanita waved toward herself. "Speak on it."

"Well, I had a vision—like a psychic vision, or whatever you call it." She paused, waiting for Vanita to correct her phrasing, but the oracle simply nodded. "And in the vision, I saw a man. He was bleeding out on the ground. There was a lot of blood and I don't think he—"

"Describe this man for me."

"Um…he was dressed very nicely. Tie. Green jacket, no overcoat. I think he had dark hair too." Samantha pinched the bridge of her nose and shook her head. "It's hard to tell because everything was so dark. It was at night...or maybe early morning. It all happened so fast—the vision. Before I could really process what was happening, it was over. I just remember seeing the blood-soaked snow in an alley or something that was lined with brick walls."

"Did he have the same complexion as me?" Vanita's skin was darker, as was her hair. Samantha guessed her ancestry was probably from southeast Asia or somewhere in that vicinity.

"I think so?" Again, Samantha cringed, hoping she wasn't remembering incorrectly. "I'm not really sure about the details."

"Long or short hair?"

"Shorter. He seemed pretty well-groomed. Like I said, he was well-dressed."

"Any idea about height or build?"

Samantha shrugged. "He seemed average height—but he was laying on the ground and there was nothing around to compare it to. He looked pretty trim."

Vanita sat back in her seat and nodded, her finger and her thumb pinching her chin.

"Do you know this man?" Samantha asked, hopeful. "My sister and I tried looking for him last night, but we couldn't find him. If you can help us—and stop whoever attacked him— maybe we can save him!"

"I believe I do know this man." Vanita closed her eyes and continued to nod.

"Who is he? *Where* is he? If he's in trouble, we need to—"

"He is my brother, Oren."

"Your brother? How can you be sure? *I'm* not even sure."

"I'm sure." Vanita let out a heavy breath. "I have been searching for him for some time. And now, it seems, he has come to find me."

"But it could be anyone."

"Sweetie, if you don't recognize this man and I was the only one locked into the reading with you, then it seems that you've channeled my connections and received the vision I was unable to receive for whatever reason."

"So the vision was meant to be, but it was meant to be for you?"

Vanita nodded.

"So I was simply the, uh, receptor to it?"

The oracle shrugged. "At least, that is my theory."

Samantha thought of her connection to Kathy. If anything were to happen to her—or if someone had suspected something was *going to* happen to her—Samantha would be hellbent on making sure she was safe. The least she could do was make sure the same was said for Vanita's brother.

"Then if that's the case, I need you to come home with me."

CHAPTER 13

Kathy lay back on the couch with the phone pressed to her ear. Her finger twirled around the cord as she talked to Jeremy. There was so much she needed to tell him about what was going on with Steven. After she had pushed herself to finish her essay, she figured she deserved a break to lay on the couch.

And she hoped she had enough time to divulge the story before Samantha and Steven arrived home.

"I *was* going to talk to Samantha about it, but I figured I'd talk to Steven instead," she said into the phone. "I want to hear his excuse directly before I take it to Samantha."

"And you said he wasn't at work today?"

"Not when I went."

"Maybe he just stepped out."

She scoffed. "That's exactly what I hope he's *not* doing. Stepping out."

"You know what I meant."

"I looked for him, too," she went on. "Went down to the cafe down the street from his office. Not there. Went to the mall to the kiosk I saw them at before. They weren't there either. I just hope they weren't shacking it up somewhere in a parking lot."

"It's twenty degrees outside," Jeremy said. "I'm sure a parked car is not anyone's first option in this weather, even with the heat on."

"True." It was something even Kathy and Jeremy hadn't tried. "But they had to be somewhere."

"The only thing you know for sure is that Steven wasn't at work. For all you know he was with a client."

"Ah, but even one of his co-workers said it was odd that he said he was stepping out to meet a 'colleague' and not a 'client.' That means no one at the office knew who he was meeting, either."

"Maybe he's arranging a gift for your sister," Jeremy reasoned. "You said she's been having some medical issues lately."

"My sister's feeling fine," Kathy said dismissively. "If you ask me, she just needs to take a day off and nap. The damn girl works so friggin' hard."

"Says the one who was just complaining about being

stressed out the other day. Perhaps you should take your own advice?"

"I will this weekend. Right now, we're talking about Samantha and Steven. I need to find out what—"

The front door opened and Kathy shot straight up. She craned her neck to look around the corner. When a woman in a purple coat filled with patches stepped into view, Kathy took note. Was this the same woman she saw Steven with? Should she hide?

Her thoughts fizzled out when Samantha stepped into view seconds later.

"Oh good, you're home," Samantha said to her. "We need to talk."

Kathy lifted the phone back to her ear. Jeremy was calling her name on the other end. "I'll call you back, Jeremy. I gotta go."

CHAPTER 14

H ere you go." Kathy handed the cup of tea to Vanita and settled beside her sister on the couch across from the newcomer.

"Thank you, dear," she said with a kind smile. "Oh my, where should I begin?"

"Start with how you know that man in my vision is your brother," Samantha said.

Kathy kept a skeptical eye on the woman. She didn't trust the fact that Samantha *just happened* to get a vision and in that vision the man *just happened* to be Vanita's brother. Samantha must be rubbing off on her, because usually Kathy was the one that was quick to trust. Perhaps her theory that Samantha just needed a nap was wrong, because bringing this woman home was definitely not normal behavior for her sister.

"To tell that story, I need to further explain something about my family," Vanita said. "My brother and I were fairly close growing up. My whole family was. In fact, my parents were kind of the pillars of our little neighborhood community."

"Did you grow up in Erie?" Samantha asked.

Vanita nodded. "We did, in a posh neighborhood near the water. I know, you must be thinking that I certainly don't *look* wealthy enough to live in such a neighborhood, but a number of years ago my whole world changed."

"You lost touch with your brother," Samantha said, filling in the gaps.

Vanita looked down into her tea, which, Kathy noticed, she had yet to take a sip from. "Well, yes. However, we fell out of touch because our parents were, uh…" She lifted her chin and looked off as emotion came over her. When she spoke again, her voice was soft, cracking. "My parents were murdered."

As much as she tried, Kathy couldn't help but feel sorry for the oracle. She and Samantha both knew that losing parents was a terrible feeling. And to lose them both at once? She couldn't imagine.

The sisters had been young when their mother died. Only Samantha had faint memories of her. But at least they had their father. For a number of years he was there, until he wasn't. He disappeared mysteriously when Kathy was still in high school and so far they had been unable to uncover the mystery of what had happened to him.

Kathy reached for a box of tissues from the table behind the couch and extended it toward Vanita, who took two to wipe away her tears.

The oracle swatted the air, trying to will away her sadness. "I'm sorry. It's been almost six years, but it's still hard."

"Of course," Samantha said. "It'll never be easy."

Vanita took a moment to compose herself, then took a deep breath and continued. "My brother and I differed on how to proceed after that. He wanted to find my parents' killer and I just wanted to move on."

"*Did* he find who did it?" Kathy asked.

She shook her head. "Not exactly. He was convinced he had tracked the killer down to a sorcerer. Apparently the sorcerer noticed the power and the status my parents had and wanted to take it away from them. But my brother was unable to find a way to stop the sorcerer himself. You see, we may be gifted as oracles, but we still can't hold a candle to a sorcerer, who has collected unknown powers."

"So what did your brother do?" Samantha asked. "Oren, right?"

Vanita nodded. "Yes, Oren. I begged him to let it be. To let the sorcerer leave us alone so that we could move on. But my brother had too much pride. He felt like he needed to avenge our parents' death. And I wasn't about to stand by and watch as another one of my family members—the last one I have left—

get killed by the very same sorcerer he was chasing."

"Not to mention you," Kathy said. "If he killed your whole family, you'd likely be next."

"Are you sure it was a sorcerer?" Samantha asked.

Vanita nodded. "Absolutely."

"Did his powers have anything to do with the weather?"

Kathy's head snapped over to Samantha. She brought her eyebrows together as she asked, "The weather? Where did that even come from?"

Samantha shrugged. "Just something I read before. I thought it might help us identify who it was."

"No, I don't believe his powers has anything to do with the weather," Vanita said.

Kathy continued to stare at her sister, surprised at where that comment had come from. What kind of magical investigations was Samantha doing without her? Then again, Kathy had her own experience with sorcerers that Samantha didn't know about because of an alternate timeline.

"So do you believe that the sorcerer is the one who killed Oren in my vision?" Samantha asked.

Vanita shrugged. "He's the only one I can think of who would want to hurt Oren. But in your vision, my brother wasn't struck down with magic, was he?"

Samantha considered. "No, I don't believe so. Then again, my vision was mostly just him on the ground, bleeding out."

"Oh, right," Vanita said with a smile.

ORACLE

"Sam, can I—" Kathy started, but Vanita cut her off.

"Yes, please. Go discuss amongst yourselves. I've certainly presented you with a lot of information and a proposition that is dangerous. I understand you need to discuss whether you would like to help me."

"How did you…?" Kathy trailed off.

Vanita smiled. "I'm an oracle, honey."

"Are you sure you don't mind?" Samantha asked.

"Not at all! Go on. I'll be right here. Take your time." Vanita cradled her tea in her hands and took a sip before leaning back in her chair to get comfortable.

CHAPTER 15

Kathy, that was a little rude to interrupt her story, wasn't it?" Samantha whispered and glanced back toward the door into the dining room. She didn't think that Vanita could hear her, but she didn't want to take any chances.

"She didn't seem offended," Kathy said. "Besides, she knew I was going to say that."

"That's not the point!"

"You're right. The point is that her story doesn't sit well with me."

The older sister hooked an eyebrow. "The murder of her parents? The threat on her family? You don't think that's something we can relate to?"

Samantha thought of Danielle Bowen in Salem, NY. It had

only been about a month since she had been in touch with her witch friend, and even though she knew she needed to back off for the sake of her own life, Samantha couldn't help but think about the similarities between Vanita's story and Danielle's. Then again, it wasn't uncommon for magical beings—especially witches—to be under the threat of other magical beings.

"Our parents weren't murdered," Kathy said pointedly. "But besides that, I think something fishy is going on."

Samantha rolled her eyes and crossed her arms. "Well what I think is that we have a woman here who needs our help. You said the same thing a couple weeks ago with Scarlett. I didn't want to help her, but it's a good thing we did. How is this any different?"

"It just is," Kathy argued. "Scarlett was innocent and had been wronged by another witch. This whole elaborate tale that Vanita is spinning just doesn't add up. First of all, you don't get visions and yet—surprise!—you got one. Second, the vision happened when you went to see an oracle for a reading. A skilled one, at that. Don't you think she could've pushed that vision on to you?"

Samantha considered it, but chose to believe what Vanita had said. "I intercepted a vision that was meant for her. The sorcerer probably put a spell on Vanita so she couldn't get any visions about her brother."

"I'm just saying, I don't want to get involved with a sorcerer, who could have a lot of power. Especially, if it turns out Vanita isn't telling the truth."

"Why would she lie about her family like that?" Samantha asked.

Kathy shrugged. "Okay, I'll give you that. I just want to be careful."

"And we will. I haven't gotten any bad vibes off of her, and don't you think I would've by now if she had any ill intentions?"

Her younger sister let out a sigh. "I guess I can't argue with your track record. You haven't heard *any* bad thoughts coming from Vanita?"

"I don't make it a habit to pop into people's minds, but no. Nothing has jumped out at me."

"Are you going to? Pop into her mind, that is."

"I don't see a need to, Kathy. If I think something might not be adding up, I'll dig around in her brain, but until then, I'm not about to invade her privacy. We need to be able to trust people. Not *everyone* is out to get us."

"Okay, but if *anything* comes up, I want you to say something to me so we can both be on alert."

"I promise." Samantha turned to return to the living room, but Kathy reached for her arm. "What is it?"

"There's something…" Kathy looked conflicted. "Um…it's about Steven."

"Did something happen?" Samantha asked. "Did he call here or something? He should be home anytime now, unless he's working late."

Kathy stared at her, then cracked a smile. "I was just wondering what he would think about this. I know how you two had that huge argument up in Buffalo."

Samantha tried not to think about that. That had been the first spat they had had as a married couple, and it had been a big one. But time had passed. They had set boundaries, and Samantha gave in to allow him to worry about her. And she agreed to see the doctor, just like he wanted. Two days from now, hopefully she'd know why she had those episodes a few weeks ago. And why she continued to feel off.

"Steven will be okay with it," she finally said. "He'll have to be. We don't really have a choice in this. This is who I am. This is what I do."

CHAPTER 16

So what exactly are you asking of us?" Kathy asked as they walked back into the living room.

"Kathy," Samantha said as a warning. She took a seat on the arm of the chair. "What she means is, how can we help you find Oren?"

"Yeah, we already tried looking for him last night and came up with bupkis," Kathy added.

"Well, I think if we combine our powers, we should be able to find him," Vanita said.

"How exactly?" Kathy pushed.

"As an oracle, my spellcasting is limited. Any spell I come up with would be confined to how my power manifests itself: through visions and readings and feelings. As witches, you are capable of a higher level of magic."

Kathy nodded. It was one of the reasons they sometimes acted as unofficial policewomen of the magical world.

"So do you just need us to cast a spell with you to locate him?" Samantha asked.

Vanita hesitated, then nodded. "Perhaps. However, spellcasting isn't even a strength of mine. I may even be doing that wrong."

Samantha looked to Kathy. "Out of all of us, my sister is the best at crafting spells."

"Would you be willing to create a spell to help me reunite with my brother?" Vanita asked with pleading eyes.

Kathy studied the woman, searching for any sign of deceit. But all she saw was sincerity. A desperate need to find a piece of her family. Kathy knew she'd be just as desperate if she were in the oracle's shoes.

"I'll see what I can do," Kathy said. "But if you needed Samantha to intercept a vision of him that was meant for you, it might not even work."

"I believe the sorcerer is cloaking my brother's location from me. You don't think your powers would be strong enough to overcome that?"

The sisters looked at each other, exchanging the same thought between them without saying a word.

"It depends," Samantha said.

"On?"

"On what powers the sorcerer has," Kathy explained. "And how skilled he is at them."

The hope seemed to fade from Vanita's eyes. "Oh."

"But I'll certainly try," Kathy added quickly. She hated that Vanita's story was getting to her. She wanted to remain skeptical in case this whole thing did go sour.

"While she's coming up with that, why don't you and I do another reading," Samantha suggested. "Maybe I can get another vision of him—or the same one—and pick up more details that I might've missed the first time. Maybe even identify the attacker."

"That would save us a ton of time." Kathy stood and started back toward the kitchen. "I'm going to get rhyming. No promises on how long this will take."

CHAPTER 17

Samantha and Vanita sat cross-legged on the floor in the large hallway between the foyer and the dining room. In front of them sat candles and herbs and mugs filled with tea leaves, all situated on an ornate knit blanket the sisters sometimes used as an altar cloth.

Both witch and oracle sat with their eyes closed and their hands clasped with one another, focusing on centering their energies and connecting to the vision that Samantha received the day before.

The house was silent. The only sounds were the occasional wind gusts outside that whistled through the old single-pane windows, and the furnace pumping in the basement, sending warm air through the ducts to combat the drafty windows.

The peace and quiet ambience was suddenly disrupted when Vanita broke the connection.

"Someone's coming," she said.

The abrupt change brought confusion to the witch. "What?"

Before the oracle could answer, the door swung open, sending cold air inside, which blew out the candles at the altar.

Samantha snapped to attention with venom in her eyes that their ritual had been interrupted. When she saw it was her husband, her anger quickly subsided.

Steven closed the door quickly behind him and bent over to pull off his snow-covered shoes and stick them on the drying rack near the door. Clad in his socks, he began to pull off the rest of his winter clothing, but stopped when he saw Vanita.

"Oh. Hi."

"Hello," Vanita said with a bashful smile.

"This is my husband, Steven," Samantha introduced. "Steven, this is Vanita. She needs mine and Kathy's help. And, not that I don't love seeing you home after a long day, but you did kind of interrupt something."

Steven pulled off his wool hat, which left his dark hair standing up all over. He began to unwind his scarf as well. "How long have you been home?"

"Like an hour or so."

"I see."

"Why?"

"Can you and I have a word?"

"Everyone wants a one-on-one pow-wow today," Samantha muttered. She rolled her eyes and then slowly rolled to her side to get to her feet. Her vision momentarily fogged and she grabbed the banister on the stairs for extra support, trying to pass it off casually. But she knew Steven noticed, even though he didn't say anything.

Steven hung his coat on the hook and started to head to the kitchen, but Samantha held out her hand to stop him.

"No, Kathy's in there writing a spell," she explained. "Let's go upstairs." She turned back to Vanita. "Sorry. I'll just be a minute. Why don't you try to get a reading on your own?"

The oracle nodded. "I will try."

Upstairs, Steven closed the door behind them when they walked into their bedroom. He sat on the edge of the bed and peeled off his socks. "So you've been home for a while?"

"Yeah. My regular time, I guess." Samantha stood by the door and hugged herself. It was a conscious effort so she didn't come across as angry, even though she was kind of annoyed that Steven had interrupted her meeting with Vanita and had insisted on talking to her in private. Couldn't he see that she was busy?

"You didn't need to stay late?" he asked.

"For what?"

"It's the beginning of tax season," he said. "I have a stack of papers on my desk that I still need to get to, but I didn't want to stay any later. I certainly could have."

Samantha shrugged. "We're a smaller firm than yours. Fewer cases to work through."

Steven sighed and shook his head as he busied himself with unbuttoning his sleeve cuffs. "Didn't you say your firm has an audit coming too?"

"What's with all these questions about my work? You act like I'm not even doing my job. I put in my full eight hours today and came home to do witch stuff."

"I just want to make sure you're not just doing the bare minimum to rush home to take care of that witch stuff."

Samantha tucked her hair behind her ears and put her hands on her hips. Now she was pissed. "Just so you know, Mr. Marsden still thinks I'm one of his best employees. And he did start to give me more work to do because I finished the taxes for the clients on my plate. I put in my time when I'm at work. I'll put in more tomorrow. But I'm not about to sacrifice my evenings just to prove my worth at work. That's a line I do not want to cross. So stop lecturing me about how to do my job."

Steven tossed his dress shirt into the hamper and put up his hands to try to calm his wife down. "I know you're a hard worker. I'm sorry for implying that you're not. But…" He looked off and let out a deep breath. "I just want you to be careful. This is your first tax season. You also still haven't seen the doctor after what happened a couple weeks ago. And I know something's still wrong with you. I saw how you stumbled downstairs just now."

She couldn't deny that, so she changed her tactic. "Are we done?"

He stepped forward and tried to hug her, but she didn't give in and held her pose. Instead, he settled for a kiss on the forehead. "I'm sorry for starting an argument when I first got home. I was just surprised to see that woman here."

"Vanita."

"And what kind of trouble is she in?"

"Her brother is in danger and she needs our help to find him," Samantha explained. When she saw his expression hadn't changed, she added, "She's an oracle."

"Isn't that like a psychic?"

"Sort of."

"And she didn't see the attack coming?"

"No. That's the problem. Someone made it so that she couldn't find her brother. Now she wants me and Kathy to help her find him before he gets hurt."

Steven pulled open a drawer in his dresser and pulled out a pair of sweatpants. "Since when are you two available for hire? I thought you mostly helped nonmagical people who were under attack? First that Scarlett girl a couple weeks ago, now this woman."

"It depends on the situation," Samantha said. "Are you done grilling me? Can I go back to helping Vanita before her brother winds up dead?"

He sighed again. "Yeah. That's fine. Go."

She turned to the door, guilty that they hadn't really resolved their argument. But there was no resolution to their situation. What he wanted, she couldn't give him. He just needed to learn to deal.

"Sam?"

"Yes?"

"What about dinner? I'd like for us to sit down and talk to each other about our day."

She shook her head. "I'm not sure how long this is going to take."

He nodded. "Okay."

As she turned away, she tried not to think about how guilty the look in his eyes made her feel. One month into their marriage and she was already neglecting her husband. When would she be able to find her balance?

CHAPTER 18

Kathy leaned against the doorframe between the dining room and the foyer. She watched as Vanita sat on the floor with her legs crossed, motionless. Her eyes were closed, her hands resting on her knees, her back straight.

It was a wonder to Kathy how someone could sit so still and so quiet for so long. She was also debating whether or not they could trust the oracle. The emotion in Vanita's voice when she was talking about her family was real. At least, it seemed that way to Kathy. And Samantha hadn't heard anything nefarious from Vanita's thoughts, either.

Still, the whole situation didn't sit well with Kathy. Something seemed off about it. Where had this woman come from? Why did Samantha intercept a vision meant for Vanita?

Why wasn't Vanita *really* able to see it?

Kathy's attention shifted to Samantha as she bounded down the stairs.

"Did I hear Steven come home?"

"Uh…yeah. He has work to do so he's probably going to stay upstairs. Is the spell ready?"

Turning to the notebook she set on the dining room table, Kathy said, "I've done the best that I can. I think it'll work. I adjusted the spell we usually use to locate people."

Vanita rose to her feet. "I haven't had any luck having a vision. However, we need to move fast. The sun has set and I fear the attack may be happening soon. I'll take any help I can get at this point, my dears."

"What do we need for the spell?" Samantha asked her sister.

"Four yellow candles and a goblet," Kathy said.

"That's it?" Vanita asked.

"The focus should be on your connection to your brother," Kathy explained. "I don't want to muddy it up with any other herbs or tools or anything that might take away from that."

Vanita nodded meekly. "Oh. Okay."

Kathy studied her. What was the aversion to a simple spell like this? One that she had just spent time writing. If Vanita thought she could do better, why hadn't she? She was certainly welcome to try. After all, she had come to them for help.

"Cool, everything should be upstairs." Samantha ran back up the stairs to retrieve the items from the cabinet where they kept the magical supplies.

Kathy and Vanita regarded each other with friendly smiles that Kathy suspected concealed mistrust on both sides. Luckily, Samantha came down moments later with the candles and the large golden basin.

"Since our other ceramic bowl was smashed a few weeks ago, I picked up this one at an occult shop over on 26th Street." Samantha set them on the dining room table. "It's about as authentic as we're going to get."

Kathy began to pull a chair out from the other side of the table, but Vanita spoke up.

"I'm sorry. But if this is such a simple spell, I must insist on sitting on the floor. We're more in-tuned to our bodies that way."

The sisters looked at each other. Samantha shrugged and grabbed the basin. "Works for me. I'm going to go fill this up with water."

Kathy cringed at being alone with Vanita again, but was glad to have the distraction as she searched through the hutch in the dining room for candle holders and a lighter. By the time she located them, Samantha was carrying the filled basin back into the foyer.

Samantha and Vanita both kneeled on the hardwood. Vanita cleared the altar they had been using to make room for the new instruments. When Kathy joined them, she arranged the candles in the direction of north, south, east, and west, and lit them each.

"Let's hold hands and repeat after me," Kathy instructed.

We call on the strength of our power,
To overcome a sorcerer's hack.
Show Oren's face in the water,
Without the magic holding us back.

The trio repeated the spell several times without any obvious indication that it had taken effect. But Kathy held firm in her effort to help Vanita and continued to repeat the spell until she heard her sister's voice.

"That's it!"

Both Kathy and Vanita opened their eyes and looked into the water, which displayed a snow-covered alley with a man laying in the center between two tire tracks.

"That's the alley from my vision!" Samantha said excitedly.

"But where is it?" Vanita asked.

"I've seen this before." Kathy closed her eyes and tried to rack her brain for where she knew it from. She had seen it in the daytime, which made this watery nighttime image difficult to decipher. She opened her eyes and studied the image again. There was a tall brick wall on one side and a one-story corrugated metal wall on the other side, which was lined with at least ten different electric meters.

"I've never paid attention to the back sides of buildings

before," Samantha mused.

"How many alleys in Erie are there anymore?" Vanita asked. "In visions of the past, I've seen hundreds of them. But nowadays—"

"I've got it!" Kathy said. "This is next to the Asian Food Mart. It's a new commercial building on French Street, but it backs up to a small little alley—I think it has a name or something." She released the other two women, which broke the connection and dissolved the image in the basin. But it didn't matter.

Back at the hutch in the dining room, Kathy searched through the drawers until she found a map of the city. Spreading it open on the dining room table, she found French Street and followed it up until she found the small street that extended from 12th and 13th between State and French.

"Commerce Street!" she said triumphantly. "*That's* where it happens!"

CHAPTER 19

The wind cut through Samantha's jacket, sending chills throughout her body. She peered around the corner of a dumpster on Commerce Street. The thoroughfare may have once been more substantial but was now just a forgotten alley. It ran behind a group of row buildings on State Street and a newly-constructed plaza on French Street. Now the alley was only used for back entrances and dumpsters.

"How much longer are we going to wait?" Kathy asked from behind Samantha. "I thought seeing it in the ritual meant it was tonight. How can we be sure it's not another night?"

"I'm sure," Vanita said from the other side of Kathy. The three of them leaned against the dumpster in a line with Samantha and Vanita at the ends.

"Shh," Samantha shushed. "If we keep blabbering and he spots us and runs off, it could alter the vision. We need to be quiet and intercept him before the attacker comes. I would like to catch the killer now, when we know where and when he's going to attack."

"We don't know *when…*" Kathy muttered.

Samantha rolled her eyes and turned back to the alley to keep an eye out. Where was Oren? The vision she got *and* the ritual both showed him here. Judging by the amount of snow on the ground and the amount of darkness, it looked like it was the correct time too.

"Do you hear that?" Kathy asked in a whisper.

Samantha nodded. "Footsteps." She looked around the corner, then turned back to her sister and whispered, "It's him. Get ready."

Kathy's time specialty would be instrumental in freezing the scene—stopping the attacker in his tracks before he could strike Oren. That way, they could get Vanita's brother to safety and take care of the attacker without the threat of Oren being injured.

Samantha didn't dare peer around the corner of the dumpster until the footsteps came closer. When she was sure he was just on the other side of the dumpster, she turned and rose to her feet.

At the same time, Vanita jumped to hers.

"What are you—?" Kathy started, but was shoved aside by Vanita.

Samantha turned to the commotion behind her to see what was happening and was stunned to see Vanita brandishing a knife.

Before either sister could react, the oracle flung the knife at her brother. Just as it had played out in Samantha's vision, the blade hit Oren's abdomen and he fell back into the snow.

"You lied to us!" Samantha shouted, outraged as Vanita raced up and snatched something hanging from around Oren's neck.

Kathy ignored her sister and sprung into action, chasing after Vanita out of the alley.

As the two disappeared around the corner, Samantha snapped out of her stupor and hurried to Oren's side. If Vanita had been lying to them—something Samantha *knew* she should've seen with her telepathy—then that must mean that Oren was the target all along. And maybe Vanita had other accomplices to come along and finish the job.

Dropping to her knees in the snow, Samantha pulled off her scarf and pressed it to Oren's side. His blood had already stained the snow that she was kneeling in, seeping into the knees of her pants.

"Stay with me," she told him. "Come on."

The last thing she wanted was to lose the man she was so adamant on protecting. Especially right after she had been fooled by his very attacker.

CHAPTER 20

Kathy jogged back to the alley, breathless and with a stitch in her side. Her nose was running, her chest was burning, and her feet were killing her. Somehow, she was simultaneously hot and cold. The snow-covered sidewalks and the whipping winds didn't help her pursuit any.

"How is he?" she asked as she joined her sister beside Oren.

"Not good." Samantha pressed a blood-soaked piece of fabric against his side, which Kathy faintly recognized as the scarf that had been around Samantha's neck only a few minutes ago. "Where's Vanita?"

"I lost her in that old industrial complex on French. No lights, probably broken glass, drug addicts, and gangbangers in there. Didn't think it was worth the risk."

Samantha nodded absently. She was too preoccupied with Oren.

"Has the bleeding slowed at all?" Kathy knew nothing about medical treatments, but at the very least she knew that bleeding that wouldn't clot was bad news. If it had slowed or stopped, he had a chance.

"I think so," Samantha said. "It's hard to tell. He needs to go to a hospital."

"I can go get the car—"

"No," the man blurted, then began coughing. He clutched his side, his hands over Samantha's bloody hands, and winced as the pain ripped through him.

"You don't really have a choice, dude." Kathy rose to her feet. "Getting the car would take too long. I'll go around front to one of those businesses on State and call for an ambulance."

"No," he said again. Firmer this time. Between ragged breaths, he went on, "No hospital. We need…to find…my sister."

"Trust me, we will," Samantha told him. "There's a score to settle now. I don't take lightly to being lied to." She turned to Kathy. "If we call 9-1-1 they're going to ask questions about the knife wound. Right now, my hands are the only ones with blood on them."

"We can't just let him bleed out here, Sam."

"I know! But what are we supposed to do?"

"Is there a magical remedy or something that you know

of?" Kathy asked. "Some kind of potion or ointment of balm that you can whip up to stop the bleeding?"

Oren broke into another coughing fit and groaned in pain.

"That's it," Samantha said. "Screw the questions—go call 9-1-1. I'm not going to let him die."

Kathy turned to head back down the alleyway, but Oren shouted for her to stop.

"No! We need to find…we need to find my…my sister."

Samantha nodded, holding firm against his wound. "Yes, we will, but—"

"She took my family's amulet." He rested his head back against the snow and tried to wet his lips, but his tongue was dry. "If she's not stopped…with the amulet…she could…wipe out the whole East Coast."

Kathy and Samantha exchanged looks. They had no other option now. Vanita needed to be stopped.

CHAPTER 21

Kathy finished cleaning up the blood that had dried from around Oren's wound. It was the best she could do to help him feel more comfortable after what she assumed was a horrible patch job on her part. Their couch was now soaked in blood, which rendered it essentially useless. So was her favorite throw blanket.

Their living room was a far cry from a hospital room.

But at least Oren was alive. For now. If he developed an infection, she wouldn't know what to do. And they needed to be on alert in case Vanita came back to finish him off. After all, she knew where the sisters lived. Clearly, she knew how to manipulate them.

Wiping her hands in the rag that she had used to clean up

Oren's wound, Kathy stepped into the kitchen, where Samantha and Steven were. She could tell she interrupted a very tense argument from the way the newlyweds looked at each other.

"Well, he's not bleeding anymore." Kathy stepped to the sink and scrubbed up to her elbows as she gave her report. "And he's asleep, which should help him heal. We just need to make sure he keeps up with his liquid intake. Can't let him dehydrate."

For someone who really didn't know much about how to treat knife wounds, she certainly sounded like she knew what she was talking about.

"So things got pretty bad out there, huh?" Steven asked. Samantha gritted her teeth. "Vanita set us up. I don't know why I couldn't see it—or hear it. I'm telepathic! I should have been able to notice the warning signs before anyone else."

"You haven't been yourself lately," Kathy said.

"And you were hyper-focused on saving that guy," Steven added.

Kathy had her back to them as she finished washing up, but the pregnant pause said enough. Samantha didn't accept the sympathy Steven offered. In an effort to ease tensions, Kathy said, "I just wonder what we should do now."

"Obviously we need to find Vanita."

Kathy shut off the water and reached for a clean towel. She turned and leaned against the sink as she dried her hands. "And we'll need Oren's help for that. If we can trust him."

"You don't think we can?" Samantha asked.

"His sister deceived us. How do we know he's not playing the same game?"

"He's the victim."

"Yes, but the perception has changed now. Up until Vanita threw that knife at him, we thought she was someone we could trust." It took everything in Kathy not to say, "I told you so," like she wanted to.

"We need to talk to him, then," Samantha said. "Get an idea of whether or not we can trust him. Hopefully my power will actually work on him."

"What you all *need* is rest," Steven cut in. "Including you, Sam. It's almost ten o'clock. It's Wednesday. You have to work tomorrow."

"Well, sorry Steven, but I can't plan when these types of emergencies come up," Samantha snapped. "Not all attacks are going to happen on the weekend."

In another effort to relieve tension, Kathy said, "I don't have class tomorrow. I was planning on spending tonight at Jeremy's—I already told him I'd be late. I could just tell him I'm not coming at all."

Nobody spoke for a moment, the tension still heavy. Finally, Steven said, "Jeremy's called several times tonight. He's been asking for you."

"Probably because I left things vague and we never made plans to reschedule," Kathy said. "I'll give him a call and come up with an excuse. I'll just work on my homework here tomorrow while everyone's at work. I'll keep an eye on Oren in the meantime. He should be sleeping most of the day anyway."

"And Vanita?" the older witch asked.

Kathy shrugged. "She partially succeeded tonight. She got the amulet from him. Even if it's as powerful as Oren says it is, it's going to take her a while to execute her plan. She's not going to make a move tonight. She's going to celebrate her win for a moment. Not to mention, *she* needs rest too."

"See?" Steven said to his wife. "Crisis averted for now."

Samantha glared at him. "Fine. We'll have find Vanita after work tomorrow then. Let's just hope she doesn't make any moves until then."

"Actually, I have to work tomorrow night," Kathy said.

"Can't you call in?"

Kathy sighed. She felt like she was always the one making the sacrifices, even though she was just as busy as Samantha. But her sister had the steady job that paid most of the bills so it was more important for her not to burn any bridges there.

"I would like to keep the hours, but I guess I could see if Leslie or someone would want to switch," Kathy said. "Maybe I can work this weekend instead."

"Well, let's hope this Vanita business doesn't stretch into the weekend. I want to find her and give her what's coming to her."

"And you don't want to miss your doctor appointment on Friday," Steven added.

Samantha didn't say anything, but the look in her eyes said

enough. Quietly, Kathy agreed with Steven. Something was off about her sister. It was time they started solving that mystery before the next crisis came up.

95

CHAPTER 22

Shoot, shoot, shoot," Kathy muttered to herself as she raced down the stairs. She had just gotten out of the shower when she heard the doorbell ring and haphazardly pulled on her clothes to answer the door. Luckily they were just sweats since she had no intention of going anywhere until later, but she noticed that she hadn't fully dried off her body and the cotton clung to her skin. Worse, her hair was still wet and leeching water down the back of her shirt.

She swung open the door, letting the frigid winter air blow in.

Jeremy stood on the other side holding a cup of coffee and a small paper bag. "Good morning," he said with a smile. "Can I come in for a second?"

Oren lay just a few feet away, still sleeping, in full view of the foyer. If Jeremy stepped inside, he would certainly have questions that she didn't have answers for. At least, not any answers that she could tell him.

She frowned. "I actually don't have a lot of time to talk."

His smile faded a bit and he took in her outfit, but didn't say what was very obviously on his mind. "That's okay. I should probably get to work anyway." He extended the bag and the coffee to Kathy. "I thought I'd bring you coffee and a muffin to make up for the fact that we couldn't get together last night. I really missed you."

Kathy's heart ached as she reached for his gifts. "That's so sweet. Thank you! Sorry I had to cancel last night."

He shrugged and offered another smile. "That's okay. People get sick. These things happen. Are you feeling better today?"

"Much better." She held up the coffee and what looked like a blueberry muffin. "These will help—and give me the energy I need to study."

"I'm glad."

"I should probably be getting started on my homework." She began to close the door—her bare toes had gone numb— but Jeremy put his hand on it to stop her.

"Do you mind if I run in to use the bathroom? The line at the coffee shop was longer than I anticipated and it's going to take me, like, twenty minutes to get to work."

"You can't," she blurted. Her thoughts were still hung up on

Vanita's betrayal the night before.

Is Jeremy testing me? she wondered. *Does he think I'm hiding something from him and he wants to scope out the house to uncover my secret? How did he learn about it? Was it Vanita? Is she telling people we're witches to distract us so she can get away with the amulet? Or plan another attack on Oren?*

Of course, Kathy knew she *was* hiding something from Jeremy. But nothing as sinister as cheating on him. Keeping her magic from him was protecting him and their relationship until she felt comfortable that she could trust him with that knowledge. And the burden of being with someone who is constantly in danger.

Kathy wondered if the cracks she was seeing in Samantha and Steven's relationship were based on the fact that she was a witch.

"I can't?" Jeremy asked. "Why not?"

"Um…the house is a mess," she said with a shrug she hoped came across as breezy. But by the look on Jeremy's face, she was failing at that miserably. "Samantha would be really upset if I let you in and saw how crazy it is in here."

"Kathy, I've been here before when it was messy," he said. "Hell, I've even stayed here for that time that you forced me to—" He stopped.

Kathy had insisted on him staying with her after Jeremy's friend Paul had died. Just before she and him had broken up the first time. It was still a murky area of their history that they hadn't fully discussed. And the fact that Kathy couldn't tell him that she was only trying to protect him from the siren only fueled the fire that caused them to break up.

"I won't tell Samantha," he finally said.

She gulped but shook her head. With Oren on the couch, there was no way for her to let Jeremy in without raising more questions—and suspicion. "I'm sorry. I'll call you later when I'm free and the house is cleaner."

He looked down at the floor as he rubbed his forehead, letting out another sigh. "Okay. I'll see you later." He gave her a quick kiss on the cheek, then turned off and waded through the snow back to his car on the street.

"Thanks for the coffee!" she called to him, but he didn't look back.

As she watched him drive off, she couldn't help but wonder if her life was destined to be lonely. How could she get close to someone if she couldn't allow them to know every part of her?

CHAPTER 23

Books and notebooks were spread out across the dining room table. Kathy sipped on the coffee Jeremy had brought her and tried to focus on her reading, but even though she read the words, the meaning was not getting into her head.

She couldn't stop thinking about what had just happened with Jeremy. Was this second shot at their relationship doomed to fail? They'd been on and off ever since they first began dating, but their breakups had always been over petty arguments. Nothing as monumental as lies they both knew were being told. Secrets didn't make for a healthy relationship. She had once been happy with a relatively shallow relationship: going to parties, hanging out, going on adventures that required only the minimal level of emotional commitment.

But now she was making changes in her life. She was in college. She was working. She was trying to contribute more to the household bills. And Jeremy was different too. He had a full-time job now. They both had responsibilities. They both wanted more from each other. Would they ever reach a point in their relationship where she could be totally honest with him? Like Samantha had been able to do with Steven.

Not that Samantha's marriage was the picture of success right now. Not only had they been arguing more—likely because Samantha was scared of whatever health issues she might be facing—but if Kathy's suspicions were correct, Steven was already stepping out on their marriage.

Kathy wished she had some kind of proof that Steven was having an affair. But even if she did, how would that conversation go with Samantha? How could she break her sister's heart?

Kathy heard groaning from the other room and looked up to see Oren finally stirring. He had slept through the hustle and bustle of the morning rush as Samantha and Steven got ready and left for work. If it weren't for the steady rise and fall of his chest, Kathy would've been worried.

"Good morning. How are you feeling?" she called over to him.

Another groan, then his eyes flickered up toward her. "Thirsty."

Knowing that her homework was not about to get done right now, she carried her coffee and muffin to the living room and sat in the chair across from Oren. She pushed the water glass on the coffee table over to him.

"Brought that out last night," she told him. "You were out like a light. Wouldn't wake up for anything."

Oren tried to sit up and only managed to move an inch or two. He settled back onto the cushions after giving in to the pain. "I hurt all over."

"Well yeah," she said. "You got stabbed by your sister. It's a wonder you're even still alive."

He was quiet and she thought he might've fallen back to sleep, but he reached for his water and drank half of it.

"I can get you more if you want," she offered. "You need to stay hydrated so your body can heal."

"I'm okay for now," he said.

Kathy ate more of her muffin. Her mind was spinning with questions she wanted to ask him. Samantha would have the same questions but she was stuck at work. Still, Kathy couldn't pass up this perfect moment in the quiet of the early morning. It was just her and Oren and there was no chance of interruptions until later that afternoon.

"So tell me why your sister tried to kill you," she said.

"It's a long story," he said.

"Hey, I have the time. And it's not like you're going anywhere anytime soon."

He grinned. "My family have been magical practitioners for generations."

"Oracles."

"Yes. Over the years, the leaders of our family were always the oldest members. Both patriarchal and matriarchal."

"Leaders?"

"The ones who have guided us through interpretations of our visions and the mission of our purpose as oracles. How much we can help people. What we can help them with. The dissemination of knowledge, if you will."

Kathy nodded. "So like the leaders of your coven?"

"Similar, yes. Our family has always been special. Our leaders have passed down an ancient amulet that was created more than a century ago. It has always been worn by whoever the leader was at that time. The strongest in our family."

Kathy recalled her knowledge of amulets. They often began as simple pieces of jewelry or mementos held by magical practitioners, but over time they slowly absorbed the residual magic their owner dispelled. If the amulet in Oren's family was as old as he said it was, and it was attached to the most powerful members of his family, then the amulet had picked up a lot of residual magic over the years.

"That amulet must pack a punch then," Kathy said.

"Yes, it does. And its strength has led to the destruction of our family."

"Greed?"

Oren nodded. "About five years ago, my grandmother passed away. She had been the keeper of the amulet, and so the amulet then came into my father's possession. We had a small following of people in our neighborhood. People who knew we could tell the future. Sure, most people thought it was simply good fun. Illusions and tricks and that kind of thing, but some knew the truth of our gifts. Our secret somehow reached a sorcerer by the name of Callum Ahmed. He saw the following my family had gained—the power we had over people who were searching for answers or reassurance that everything was going to work out. As a sorcerer, he wanted that control. That level of authority. That power."

Kathy had only recently learned how sorcerers were drunk with a desire for power. She knew all too well the lengths they would go to to get more power.

"So Ahmed came to see my father for a reading," Oren went on. "And, of course, he noticed the amulet around my father's neck. Two days later, in the early morning hours, Ahmed returned and killed both my parents in their beds, all to steal the amulet."

Kathy's jaw dropped, although she had seen that part of the story coming. "I'm so sorry."

Oren's eyes dropped down for a moment. "Thank you."

"I know what it's like to not have any parents," she offered quietly. "My mother died before I really got a chance to know her." She took a deep breath and released it slowly before adding, "And my father simply disappeared one day six years ago. My sister and I still have no idea where he went, but we haven't heard from him and haven't been able to reach him—even magically—so I think it's a safe bet that he's dead too."

"The loss of a parent isn't something we get over easily," he said. "And losing both?" He shook his head.

Not wanting to dwell on their losses anymore, Kathy shifted the conversation back on track. "So…how do you know it was Ahmed who took the amulet from your father?"

Oren closed his eyes as he recalled the memory. "I was the one who answered the door when he first came to visit my father. I still remember seeing the evil in his eyes. It chilled me right to my soul, that look. So when I woke up that morning and discovered that my parents had been killed, I knew exactly who had done it."

"So how did you get the amulet back?" Kathy wasn't keen on facing off against another sorcerer. Especially if they also needed to track down Vanita.

"I managed to find him," Oren said. "It took months, but I finally found Ahmed and made him suffer the same fate he gave my parents. By killing him, I avenged their deaths. And took possession of the amulet, restoring what was rightfully my family's."

"I guess I can't see why Vanita would want to kill you. Wouldn't she be just as happy that you got your family's amulet back?"

"As I said, it is tradition for the oldest member of my family to be the keeper of the amulet. Since I am older than Vanita, that means I am the rightful keeper and have full access to the power held within the amulet."

"And Vanita wants the amulet for herself?"

Oren nodded. "And that is why I found it necessary to cloak myself from her. It wasn't enough to simply cut ties from her. I needed to become invisible to her, even magically."

Kathy sighed. "And we helped her find you by using our magic to work around yours."

"You didn't know."

"Yeah." Then a thought occurred to her. "Why should I believe your story when Vanita fed us a different sob story and then turned on us? Samantha and I have enough problems in our lives without getting stuck in a sibling rivalry."

"This is much more than a sibling rivalry."

"True. This is a power struggle. The root of that power is the amulet. So, if you ask me, that amulet should be destroyed."

"That amulet has always been used for good," he argued. "It is my family's duty to protect it. Yes, we are faltering in that duty currently, but we have faltered before and have always persisted. We will again this time. The thirst for power is nothing new. I will get it back and the amulet will continue to help people seeking answers. Don't destroy the potential good it could do because of one setback."

"It's a pretty big setback."

"Maybe so, but I'm confident I can make things right. The question is, are you willing to help?"

"How do I know you're not lying to me like your sister did?"

Oren paused, searching for the right way to begin. "Somewhere along the way, my sister became corrupt. It is my belief that Ahmed only visited my father after Vanita told him of the amulet's power."

"Why would she do that?"

"She wanted the amulet for herself."

"But, like you said, you're still older than her. So you'd be the keeper of the amulet."

"Perhaps she thought I'd be willing to share. Or maybe she thought she could kill me herself and she'd be the rightful keeper of the amulet. Either way, I know she underestimated the power of Ahmed as a sorcerer. She believed she could kill him to steal the amulet back. She could not."

"But you could."

"Because I am the rightful keeper. My efforts were supported by good intentions and the spirit of my lost family."

Kathy sipped her coffee, still not sure she believed everything he said based on what just happened the night before. But she had a better feeling about him than she had with Vanita.

"Keep in mind," he said, "oracles are not evil by nature. We're people, just as witches are, who sometimes make the worst decisions for the best reasons. Unfortunately, Vanita's ideals have been warped somewhere along the way."

CHAPTER 24

- JANUARY 1983 -

The room was peacefully quiet as Vanita soaked in the winter sun's rays in the sunroom of her family's home. It was her favorite place to meditate. The warmth from the sun, the separation from the rest of the house, the view out into their neighborhood with the tree-lined streets. Even without the leaves, it was beautiful.

Vanita breathed in a deep breath, feeling herself relax as she slowly exhaled. She sat cross-legged on the carpet, relying on her senses to be purely in the moment, feeling every sensation hitting her body. Meditating helped her find clarity to use her ability and find her path forward.

Everyone in her family meditated several times a day. It was something her parents had instilled in Vanita and her brother from an early age. They didn't have time-outs, they had meditations and reflections. Her father told her it was what made them special: the fact that they were so self-aware that they realized how much they needed to use their magical gifts to serve other people.

Vanita never thought anything of it. She thought everyone did that—and that everyone's parents invited other people from the neighborhood over to meditate with them. It wasn't until Vanita went to school that she realized how different her family was. But it was something she embraced. Why be just like everyone else when you can be different?

When visitors did come to meditate, it was often in the presence of the leaders of their family—Vanita's parents, now that her grandparents had passed away. Visitors were looking for a vision or a prophecy or something that could help shed insight into their uncertain future.

Sometimes, during meditations, Vanita or someone in her family would receive a vision of something that could help someone. A fall that could be avoided. A medical test that could find a potentially fatal ailment early enough. Or even a car accident that could seriously harm someone.

Vanita's father said it was their duty as oracles to share this information with the subjects of their visions. So it was important to stay connected to the community to share these visions and help people.

The sun shifted and shone right in Vanita's eyes, breaking

her concentration. She tried to ignore it, but the burning through her eyelids was too much to bear. Besides, she had already been meditating for nearly twenty minutes. She could end this session a bit early in favor of a longer one later.

She rose to her feet and wandered back into the main part of the house, being careful to keep quiet. This was supposed to be the time that the whole family meditated and if Vanita was the reason someone broke concentration—especially if they were on the verge of a vision—there would be hell to pay. More meditations and reflections.

Everyone each had their own corners of the house to meditate. Her mother chose the formal living room. Her father chose his office. Her brother, Oren, typically went into the library. And Vanita nearly always chose the sunroom.

The house was supposed to be quiet during meditation, which was why Vanita found it odd to hear voices coming from her father's office.

Crossing the great room, Vanita stood at the end of the hall leading to his office, where the door was slightly open. From here, she could hear the conversation.

"…will blow up huge," her father, Ruben, said. "Trust me on that. Invest now. It'll dip a little next week and you'll be tempted to pull out, but don't sell. Next month our shares will skyrocket."

"And we get a sixty-forty split?"

"I'll let you take the larger split," Ruben said. "Even at forty percent, we're talking an incredible amount of money."

Vanita peered around the corner to see if she could see who her father was talking to. She just caught the back of the stranger's head. He had dirty blond hair and wore a white dress shirt. He leaned back in the chair in front of Ruben's desk with a casualness that spoke to his level of comfort with Ruben.

"Exactly," the man said, "and with the bets we have in Buffalo, Cleveland, and Pittsburgh, we're going to be rich!"

"I want you to pull out of those," Ruben said. "Or see if you can place the bet under someone else's name."

"What! Why?"

"I don't want anyone getting suspicious as to why we're making all of this money," Ruben said. "We have to be careful, Clark. If we're going to continue to have these large paydays, we can't let anyone accuse us of foul play."

Clark! Vanita knew she knew him! He was their neighbor from across the street. Usually he and her father would chitchat getting the mail. On occasion, Ruben invited Clark over for a cookout in the summer, but Vanita thought they were just acquaintances. Neighbors making polite small talk. Now, it seemed, they were in business together.

And dirty business, as it was. How dare her father tell them they need to be righteous and virtuous with their ability to see the future when he was using his own gift to make money! Her blood boiled at the thought of being lied to. Worse, she felt stupid for so fully believing everything that she had been told.

Turning away from her father's office, Vanita raced toward

the formal living room. She needed to tell her mother of the sham that was their life.

CHAPTER 25

Samantha knocked on the door to Mr. Marsden's office before opening it to peek her head in. "Hi, do you have a second?"

"Not much, actually." Marsden typed on his computer, referring back to the papers spread in front of him. The device took up half of his desk, but it was the latest technology in computing numbers. All of the other major accounting firms had at least one. Samantha, however, still only had an electric typewriter, but Steven's office had several computers.

"This will only take a second."

He typed in another set of numbers, marked his place on the paper, then waved her in.

"I just wanted to give you an update on where I stood." She

stood behind the chair in front of his desk. "The packages for our annual accounts are ready to be mailed out to the IRS in tomorrow's mail. I've already talked to most of my clients and gotten their approval and signatures. I'm waiting on signatures from three more people, but I should have those by tomorrow and we can send those out in Monday's mail. I've also started working on some of the new accounts that came in, but I'm waiting on receipts and call backs before I can move forward with those accounts."

Samantha dished out the work she had done over the last week to make it sound better when she asked what she really came in here for: to leave early. As she crunched numbers and verified paperwork and made calls to clients, she couldn't help but wonder where Vanita had run off to. What she had taken. How Oren was doing.

Not to mention, how much of a head start Vanita was getting if she decided to leave town.

The sooner she could get home, the better. But, she also knew that Steven was right. This was tax season—the reason CPAs existed this time of year—and it wouldn't be over until April 15th, when taxes were due. Even then she suspected she'd be busy applying for extensions for some clients. Still, just because it was her busy season at work didn't mean she shouldn't be expected to live a life or manage her other responsibilities.

"You've done great work, Samantha," Mr. Marsden said with

a smile. "Thank you. I really do appreciate your tenacity and attention to detail. And actually, I'm glad you were able to get ahead a bit with your caseload because, unfortunately, I'm going to have to dump more work on you."

Samantha's smile faded.

Mr. Marsden gathered a stack of folders from the table behind his desk and passed them to Samantha, who stumbled under the sudden weight of it all.

"I'm sorry about this," he said, "but you're one of my best workers here and I know this will get done right if you set the precedent. We're being audited and the paperwork is enough to fill this whole office. If you could get a good chunk of this done while you're waiting for call backs, I'd really appreciate it."

She forced a smile. "I'll just…I'll get right on this."

"Thanks, Samantha. Like I said, I really appreciate it. And sorry again. I know it must feel like I'm punishing you for being a good worker, but I know I can trust you with it."

"No problem." She carried the stack of folders back to her desk. Flopping into her seat, she thumbed through some of them.

Looks like she wasn't going anywhere until quitting time. And even then, she should probably stay late to finish all of her work.

So much for leaving early.

CHAPTER 26

This was a line Kathy thought that she would never cross. But she was stuck with uncertainty until she had some proof. With Samantha and Steven both at work and Oren asleep downstairs, Kathy snuck into her sister's bedroom to look for proof of any affair Steven might be having.

The young witch stepped across the threshold into Samantha's room and paused. Ordinarily, she wouldn't think much of it to come and go from her sister's room whenever she pleased. But right now she was being sneaky and it didn't sit well with her. Even though she knew it was for Samantha's best interests, it still didn't feel right. For the most part, the sisters didn't keep secrets from each other.

Except, now it wasn't just Kathy and Samantha. Steven lived

here too. Sure, he had been coming around a lot before they got married, but he was officially moved in now. This wasn't just Samantha's room anymore. It was Steven's too. And the fact that she was in here to sneak through his things didn't help any.

Pushing all of that aside, Kathy started under the bed. She moved around a tote of wrapping paper, a forgotten sock, and loads of dust bunnies, but otherwise came up with nothing.

If Steven's hiding something, he wouldn't keep it in plain sight, Kathy thought. *It'd be hidden somewhere where Samantha wouldn't accidentally find it.*

That brought her attention to the nightstand on his side of the bed. She reached for the drawer and was nervous about what she might find by opening it. When she peered inside, though, she was surprised to find only a stack of books related to accounting and tax laws and a notepad and paper with simple financial calculations. Beneath the notepad was a folded section of the Saturday paper. The real estate section.

Kathy stared at it, surprised. But she remembered that Steven had taken Samantha to see that townhouse a couple weeks ago without her knowing. Samantha wasn't happy about that and it caused some tension between the newlyweds. Perhaps that was what drove Steven into the arms of another woman? Still, it wasn't proof of anything other than Steven's desire to buy a house.

Putting everything carefully back where it was, Kathy closed the drawer and stepped over to Steven's dresser.

Again, she hesitated. Rifling through her brother-in-law's sock and underwear drawer was not something she wanted to do, but certainly made a good hiding place.

Before she crossed another line that she didn't want to cross, Kathy scanned the top of Steven's dresser. There was a glass container that once held a candle the sisters had burned out, the remnants of the wax still clung to the bottom of the container. It was half full with loose change, which could easily be worth five or ten dollars if it was counted.

Beside the collection of coins were loose pieces of paper— notes and phone numbers and dates to remember. If Kathy got desperate, she reasoned, she could check the numbers in the phone book and the dates with the calendar. See if they were for anything significant. Right now, though, she was looking for obvious signs of an affair.

The rest of the dresser held knickknacks. A watch. An outdated driver's license. Pens and papers clips. Lint and dust.

It was all nothing of interest. That meant there was only one other place left to look: his dresser drawers.

Again, she debated whether she wanted to go down this road, but reminded herself that Samantha wouldn't even entertain the notion that Steven was cheating on her unless Kathy had proof. And Kathy wanted something to prove her own suspicions wrong so she wouldn't tarnish her impression of Steven.

More than anything, Kathy wanted an innocent explanation

for what she had seen at the mall. And for Steven's absence at work yesterday.

Pulling open the top drawer, Kathy tried her best to ignore the unmentionable half and dug around through the clean socks. In the back of the drawer, she felt something stiff and reached for it.

A realtor's business card.

Maureen Harlow.

Pictured on the front was the same blonde she had seen Steven with at the mall.

Immediately, Kathy began judging the woman, comparing her to Samantha. From the amount of makeup plastered on Maureen's face, it was obvious she was obsessed with her looks. Probably conceited and stuck-up. Maybe even a homewrecker.

Samantha was smarter.

Samantha was more mature.

Samantha was overall better than *Maureen Harlow*.

Looking over at the nightstand where the real estate section of the newspaper was, Kathy had a disheartening thought. Steven hid the business card in his sock drawer and didn't put it in his nightstand because he didn't want Samantha to find it. Meaning he didn't want Samantha to know about *Maureen Harlow* but he still wanted to have this floozie's number on hand for bootie calls.

Kathy's heart sunk as a realization hit her: *This* was the proof she had been looking for.

CHAPTER 27

Samantha hooked the phone between her shoulder and her ear when she answered it at her desk.

"Darius Wilcox, CPA, this is Samantha Harper, how can I help you?"

She didn't even have time for her lunch break—she was currently working through it—let alone take a phone call. But the firm was still a fairly small company and needed to answer every call and take every new client. Maybe someday Samantha would have an assistant or a secretary to take her calls. Maybe someday she'd have her own firm named after her.

"Sam, it's me," Steven said on the other end. "Just thought I'd call you at lunch."

She scoffed. "Lunch? What's that?"

"I take it you're a little busy?"

"Swamped." She lowered her voice and said, "I'm such a *terrific* worker that I get even more work as a thank you. Couldn't I just get a check?"

"You are getting a paycheck," he said. "And I'm sure this extra work will pay off with a raise when it comes time for your annual review in June."

She sighed. "I know. I'm just a little cranky with all of this audit stuff."

"I guess you're not able to leave early like you wanted to."

Samantha had mentioned it to Steven over coffee earlier that morning. She was hoping to take a half day and get a jump start on tracking down Vanita. The oracle who had betrayed them just last night wasn't even on her radar anymore with all of the work currently spilling over her desk.

Yet the need to track her down was still present. And being reminded of it only added to Samantha's stress and frustration.

"No, I'm not," she said. "I went in to ask, but he started talking about how much he appreciated me and how great I was and…" She trailed off, her eyes drifting to the window near her cubicle. "Anyway, I figured I couldn't ask after he gave me the audit stuff to start on."

"That's probably a fair assumption. It's just that time of year for our industry. The spring is always busy."

"Yeah, I know that," she said. "And I've been expecting that, it's just…it's kind of coming at the worst time."

"Life happens when you're planning other things," he said. "How are you feeling, though? We're not going to have another episode, are we?"

"Stomach's still a little off and I have a dull headache. Oh, and I'm wiped out. Like, I could probably go to bed right now and sleep until morning."

"Then maybe you should eat something good for you. And drink more water. Stay hydrated."

"I haven't touched my lunch."

"Then eat it!" he said with a chuckle. "As much as I want you to come home and relax, I'm going to assume that tonight I'm kind of on my own because of what you need to take care of with your sister?"

Samantha made a face and looked down at the spreadsheet spread out on her desk. "Yeah, sorry. After we take care of this, I'll make it up to you."

"Oh, I like the sound of that."

She smirked and rolled her eyes. "I meant, we'll have a date night."

"We can have date night after you've had a good night sleep. And when you're feeling better. We don't have to go out. Staying in and watching a movie is okay with me. We can kick Kathy out to Jeremy's for a night."

"I'm sure she'll be there anyway," Samantha said. "Anyway, I should get back to work. If it wasn't for the whole Vanita business, this would probably be a late night for me here at the office."

"You have a lot going on."

"Tell me about it. I just wish this audit were saved for the summer or something later when I had less of a workload here."

"There's always something happening," he said. "Especially with your...*eccentricities*. Unfortunately, you're just going to have to learn to deal with it."

She sighed. "I know."

The problem was, she was already spread too thin.

CHAPTER 28

Kathy finished reading over her paper just as Oren began stirring. Even with her mind racing with what she had found in Steven's dresser, she knew she needed to get focused and get the paper done. Not doing it would only lead to further stress later.

"Well good morning again, sleepy head."

He smirked, then cringed as he shifted to get comfortable. By the look on his face, no position was particularly satisfying.

"I take it you're not feeling any better?" she asked.

"The pain I can manage." He finally sunk back against the pillows. "But the pang in my stomach is putting me over the edge. Mind if I raid your fridge?"

"Absolutely, I mind." She shot to her feet. "You shouldn't be getting up. I'll fix you something to eat and bring it to you."

She walked to the kitchen and made two sandwiches with the luncheon meat that Samantha and Steven usually took for their lunches. She grabbed a bag of chips from the cupboard and carried the plate back out to the living room.

After she set the loot on the coffee table, she stood beside Oren on the couch and offered her hands. "Here, let me help you up."

He took her hands and eased himself up into a sitting position, cringing in pain. He took several deep breaths and then settled back against the cushions. "Okay. Okay. I'm all right."

Kathy handed him his sandwich. "It's a wonder you didn't need stitches. Then again, if I know my sister, she probably slipped some sort of herbal remedy into your water last night to help you heal."

Oren smiled. "So she drugged me?"

She shrugged. "She's done it to all of us at one point or another."

He laughed, then clutched at his side. "Oof! Don't make me laugh! My sides are already splitting open."

Kathy knew she shouldn't laugh, but she couldn't help it.

"This is good," he said with a mouthful, holding up his sandwich.

"Thanks. I'm quite the chef."

"You cook?"

She shook her head. "I was kidding. I'm not really one to do anything in the kitchen. My sister is much better at that kind of stuff, although neither of us are exactly chefs."

He nodded and took another bite.

Kathy finished chewing her own sandwich, then asked, "So you said your parents died about five years ago?"

"That's right."

"So what did you do before then? What was it like having parents who were known oracles?"

He shrugged. "It's how we got by."

"What do you mean?"

"They offered their fortune-telling services to the neighborhood for a fee," he said. "And those people had money to spend. They were very much the yacht club-type."

"They *gave* you money?" Kathy asked around her mouthful. She wiped some of the mayo onto what was left of her bread roll. "Like a cult?"

"Not like a cult. Like a psychic-for-hire."

"That's how Samantha met Vanita."

"It's what my sister knew from growing up."

"True. But I just can't wrap my head around the fact that your parents made yacht club-level money telling fortunes to rich people," she said.

"They made most of their money through investments and racing bets and things like that," he explained. "Things they could foresee."

"But that's an abuse of power." Kathy knew that if she exploited her own magic for fame and fortune that eventually she would feel guilty and a little dirty for having cheated the system. Misfortune would soon follow, as was typically the case with that kind of magic.

"Moral or not, it's how we lived," he said with another shrug. "Not that it matters now. They're dead."

Perhaps cheating caught up with them, Kathy thought, then instantly regretted it. Oren seemed like a very nice man. Someone who had lost his family due to greed and murder. She shouldn't be damning the dead.

"Sorry," she said. "I didn't mean to bring up bad feelings about your parents."

"It's fine. They were people. They had flaws, just like the rest of us."

"I still don't want to disrespect them."

He smiled. "It's okay. I understood what you meant."

"So what did their fortune-telling services include?"

He finished his sandwich and set the paper plate aside on the couch. With his injuries, it was too much of an effort to stretch to set it back on the coffee table. "Predicting the future, palm readings, aura readings, aura cleansings, the occasional seance, sometimes even different types of therapies with meditating and relaxation techniques. I think what kept people coming back was that my parents were friendly to talk to."

"And did you pick up any of their traits?"

"Are you looking to employ my services?"

She shrugged and smirked. "Well, I mean, we did save your life. I thought I might be able to get *something* for that effort."

"I suppose that means I could waive your fees this once." He grinned at her. "What is it that you need?"

"Well," she started to divert from the flirtatious tone between them, "I'm looking for advice from an unbiased party."

"What's the situation?"

"I'm seeing this guy who is now back in my life," she explained. "Jeremy. He's not magical in any way and doesn't know that this whole world of ours exists. I haven't told him I'm a witch."

"Most people keep their magic a secret," Oren said. "It's how we're able to do the work we're destined to do."

"Right, but I hate lying to him. And I know that this is the way it's going to have to be until I can trust him enough, but secrets don't make for healthy relationships. I mean, when Samantha told her husband she was a witch they almost broke up."

Not that the current state of Samantha's marriage was anything Kathy wanted to emulate.

"Sounds like you've already made peace with this area of your life," Oren said. "You don't like it, but you know this is the way it has to be."

"Yeah." She set her plate on the coffee table and settled back into her chair.

"Pardon my being forward, but it seems as though that that's not what's really bothering you."

She sighed, studying her nails, debating if she wanted to dive into this with a perfect stranger. But maybe a perfect stranger was just what she needed.

"You're right. Jeremy's not what's really bothering me." She debated a moment longer, wondering if it was her place to air Samantha's dirty laundry to Oren. But chances are, if he was an oracle, he may have seen it for himself anyway.

"My sister, Samantha, and her husband, Steven, just got married about a month ago—a month ago two days ago," she said. "Anyway, I saw him the other day at the mall with a woman he seemed very...*comfortable* with."

"You suspect an affair?"

"Yes! And I don't know if I should tell Samantha. I tried to look for evidence of his affair. You know, love notes or phone numbers or something. I did find this woman's business card that he had hidden, but I'm still not sure if I should tell Samantha. I mean, I don't really *know* anything for sure."

"But you're trying to protect her."

"Exactly."

"As hard as it may be, I would encourage you to get it all on the table with your sister," he said. "You two seem very close. Use that connection the two of you share to break the news to her gently. And do it quickly. The longer you wait, the more pain she will feel."

"But what if she's mad at me?"

"I'm sure she will be. Especially because you went snooping in their bedroom."

Kathy dropped her gaze down to her nails again. "You heard me upstairs?"

"I'm an oracle."

"Oh. Right."

"And it's also an old house."

She grinned. There was something so easy about talking to Oren.

"But my point is," he went on, "if your sister truly cares for you, she will see that you were only trying to protect her and she will forgive you. In time."

She sighed. "I kind of figured you'd say something like that. And honestly, I came to that conclusion on my own. I just wish there was another way."

"Sometimes loving someone means having to hurt them a little to help them in the long run."

CHAPTER 29

- JANUARY 1983 -

"Mother!" Vanita called as she rounded the corner into the front living room. It was a pristine room with white carpet, two large white plush couches facing each other, separated by a glass coffee table. Each and every day, it looked as though it was ready to be on the cover of a magazine, which meant that very rarely did anyone ever step foot in the room.

Rebekah, however, sat beneath the front window, facing the rest of the house. She had said before that she liked to have her back to a wall whenever possible because it made her feel safer. More secure in being able to watch what everyone else was doing so no one could sneak up on her. In that security, Rebekah was better able to focus her energy on meditation. The clean, white room helped ease her mind as well.

"Vanny, dear, I'm meditating. Please give me—"

"Mother, *your husband* is making bets and investments using his oracle abilities!"

Rebekah's face went from annoyed to caught. "Oh."

"Oh? Did you know about this?"

"Well…" Rebekah gestured to the house. "We don't have regular day jobs, honey. How did you think we could afford all of this?"

"I just thought you made money from clients."

She scoffed. "Please, that's hardly enough to pay the grocery bills in this house. No, the bulk of our money comes from investments that your father foresees in his visions."

"And you bring in people from the street to invest with you?" Vanita asked. "What about using our powers for the greater good? What about serving people? What about not abusing the gifts we've been given?"

"Yes, that is all true. But we also need to be able to take care of ourselves. Your father and I need to be able to provide for you and your brother."

"Look around, mother! This home is way more than our basic necessities! You and father have both let greed consume you! And you're bringing the neighbors into this, all while telling me and Oren to live the most altruistic lives that we can. It's all a lie!"

Rebekah reached her daughter to give her a hug, but Vanita pushed her away. "Calm down. Let's discuss this."

"There's nothing to discuss, mother! Father has been pretending to be someone he isn't. And if you've been going along with this charade all along, then you're not better than he is. You're both *spineless* with no morals!"

"Vanita!" Rebekah offered a sad look. "We never meant to hurt you."

"Well, you did."

"What's going on in here?" Ruben suddenly appeared from the back of the house. He looked between his wife and his daughter. "What's all the arguing about? We're supposed to be meditating."

"Sounds like you were making deals during your *meditation*," Vanita snapped. "How much money are you about to make next month, Father?"

"She overheard you talking to Clark," Rebekah explained.

Ruben sighed and his shoulders drooped. "So you've discovered how we've really been making our money?"

"Yeah, I did," Vanita said. "And now I know just how much of a shallow, fake, hollow man you are." After seeing the hurt look on her father's face, she turned to her mother. "That goes for both of you!"

"Vanny, please," Rebekah called.

"Just hear me out," Ruben said.

Vanita ignored them both and stormed out of the room.

CHAPTER 30

Kathy handed Oren a fresh glass of water just as Samantha and Steven stepped through the front door later that afternoon.

"Both came home at the same time?" she asked.

Samantha glared at Kathy. "It's been a long day."

"Someone's first tax season is hitting her hard," Steven added with a smirk.

Kathy hesitated, then decided to go for it. "Is that where you were, Steven? Working late on taxes?"

That got confused looks from both of the newlyweds.

"What else would I be doing?" he asked.

"Nothing. I just—could we talk in private?"

Samantha looked over at Oren, then stepped toward the

kitchen. "Sure, let me just—"

"Not you, Sam." Kathy put a hand on her sister's shoulder to stop her. "I was talking to Steven."

Her talk with Oren had emboldened her to speak up. But she still wanted to check with Steven first before she brought her suspicions to Samantha's attention. Then again, this current conversation was not shaping up to how she had played it out in her head.

"What's going on?" Samantha asked, looking between her husband and her sister.

Kathy considered lying. She looked over at Oren and his words echoed in her head: *Sometimes loving someone means having to hurt them a little to help them in the long run.*

As it stood, if it were true that Steven was having an affair, the only person in the room who didn't know about it was Samantha. And that wasn't fair. Better to dive right into it. Rip it off like a Band-Aid.

She pulled Maureen Harlow's business card out of her pocket and handed it to Steven. "Do you want to explain what this is about?"

He took the card and studied it, crinkling his brow. "Where did you get this?"

"Answer the question," Kathy said with an edge to her voice.

"Kathy, what's going on?" Samantha asked, trying to look around Steven's shoulder to read the card. "Who is that?"

"I saw you hugging her at the mall," Kathy said, her eyes still locked on Steven. "Tuesday, in the middle of the day when you were supposed to be at work."

Frustrated, Samantha snatched the card out of Steven's hand and looked at it closely. Her jaw jutted out in anger. "Somebody *better* start talking."

Steven looked between the two women, then looked over to Oren for help. The oracle, however, was smart enough to keep quiet.

"Maureen is someone I went to high school with," he finally said.

"And someone you've been *sleeping* with?" Samantha asked.

"Of course not!" he said. "Sam, I love you. I wouldn't have married you if I had any doubts."

"Then why are you hiding this from me?" Samantha asked.

"I found it in your sock drawer," Kathy added.

Samantha turned to her sister. "What were you doing in his—you know what? Never mind. One problem at a time." She tucked her hair behind her ears and looked to her husband. "I'm waiting for an answer."

Steven indicated the card. "You know, I had that on the top of my dresser for a week. It was right there, out in the open. It must've fallen in my dresser when I dumped the basket of clean socks in the drawer."

Likely story, Kathy thought.

"Still waiting," Samantha said.

He sighed and looked between the sisters. "Maureen has her

own realty business and her account came across my desk. I recognized the name and I needed to call her to ask her some questions about last year's expenses. *She* suggested we go for coffee so we could catch up. But it was just coffee. That's it."

"Oh." Samantha's tone softened. "So why did you keep it from me? Why be sneaky about it?"

"I wasn't trying to," he said. "But I guess I wasn't as honest as I should've been. It's just that when Maureen and I were talking, I mentioned how I would like to buy a house and she got really pushy about sending me listings. Some of them looked pretty good so I wanted to check them out, but I know we discussed staying here…" He shrugged. "I just thought it'd be easier to not say anything about it unless something perfect came up. You've been under a lot of stress and I didn't want to be the cause of more of it."

Samantha stared at Maureen's picture and sighed heavily. "So even though we discussed *not* looking for a house just yet, you ignored that and kept looking anyway."

"No, Sam, that's not—"

Kathy felt like this conversation had shifted to something different than she thought. Not only was Steven *not* having an affair, but she looked like a fool for snooping through his things. And now Steven and Samantha were arguing, even despite the innocent mistake.

Kathy regretted ever assuming that Steven was having an affair. She had created a cloud of distrust between him and

Samantha and she wondered how long it would last before they stopped worrying if getting married had been a mistake. Was this just newlywed remorse? Or was this the sign of a marriage destined to fail?

"Maybe Oren and I should go in the—" Kathy started.

"No, *you* started this," Steven snapped at her.

"Oh, so now you're mad at her for finding out your dirty little secret?" Samantha raised her voice. "Were you ever going to tell me about this Maureen woman?"

"Of course I was! When things calmed down a little bit with tax season and your witch stuff and everything."

"Do you even know who you married, Steven? Things don't *calm down* for me! And this has nothing to do with the fact that you *lied* to me when you agreed to stay here. You apparently still have one foot out the door. You don't seem to get why this house is important to us."

"*You* said you might want to move if Kathy can finally hold down a job and pay the bills," he said.

"Hey!" Kathy chimed in. "I've been at my job for almost six months now. *And* going to school!"

"Making minimum wage at that job and you still haven't declared a major," he said. "Big whoop."

"Don't get nasty with her just because you're mad that I found out," Samantha said. "This whole thing is because *you* decided to start our marriage off with lies."

"Don't even get me started about lies," he said. "Or have you forgotten the biggest secret you kept from me right up until a few months before we got married? And what would've happened if I didn't propose? Would you have told me at all?"

"You just hate the fact that I'm a witch."

He nodded. "It's annoying, yeah. I wish you weren't sometimes."

Samantha opened her mouth to retort, but bit back her reply. Kathy knew what she was feeling. Steven's words rejected a big part of Samantha's life. It was almost as if he were rejecting her. It was the unspoken fear both sisters shared. Whether someone was going to accept them even after they knew their secret. Steven's words seemed to only bring those fears to life.

"Perhaps," Oren said quietly from the couch, "we put this discussion on hold until we've all taken a break and calmed down?"

Kathy nodded. "I agree. After all, we still need to find Vanita."

But the look Samantha and Steven exchanged still conveyed an aura of distrust and hurt. Those very feelings were the ones that Kathy had stirred up. She was afraid that she had just destroyed her sister's marriage. And, despite what Oren had said, she couldn't see how this would help Samantha in the long run.

CHAPTER 31

The sisters sat on the coffee table in front of Oren and held his hands as they all chanted over a bowl of water and a couple yellow candles. It was a very crude altar, but after the argument that had just been cut short, none of them were in the mood to work hard at building an altar.

We call on the strength of our power,
show Vanita's face in the water.

They had already chanted it three times to no avail. The water continued to sit in the bowl, lifeless.

"Again," Kathy said.

Squeezing their hands tighter together, the trio recited the spell again and again and again.

Still nothing.

"This is useless." Samantha groaned and shot to her feet. She walked around the back of the blood-soaked couch and looked through the curtains onto the street.

"Because you actually need to *focus*, Sam."

"I *am* focusing!" she snapped.

Kathy took in a deep breath. Clearly, their magic wasn't working because they were not centered. They were not rested and relaxed. As much as magic had become a reflex for the sisters, it was still something that sometimes needed ideal conditions to happen successfully.

"Okay, well is there an herb or something we can add to this to help make it stronger?" Kathy asked. "Something that might compensate for the fact that none of us are on our A-game right now?"

"You can't just throw some plants at a spell and make everything better, Kathy."

The younger sister bit her lip to hold in her response. Nothing that she said to Samantha right now would be nice. Besides, they needed to find Vanita. If nothing else than to distract Kathy from the fact that her accusation seemed to cause huge problems for Samantha and Steven.

"Well, the longer Vanita is out there, the more damage she can possibly do with that amulet." Kathy turned to Oren. "And she knows the full extent of its power?"

He nodded. "Oh yeah. Of course. That's why she was so insistent on finding it and taking it for herself. Why she was willing to kill for it."

Kathy waved her hands at both Oren and Samantha. "All right. We need to try again."

Samantha didn't move. Her gaze was still out the window onto the dark street. "We've already tried it several times."

"And we'll try it again and again until it works."

"We're only going to get more aggravated and waste more time," Samantha said. "This is pointless."

"What other option do we have, Sam?"

The room was quiet as Kathy's question hung in the air. They were outsmarted, betrayed, and hurt in more personal ways than they had ever felt before. Kathy knew that her sister wanted nothing more than to hash it out with Steven right now. But, like Kathy, she was bound by her duty as a witch. As much as Steven needed her, stopping Vanita was more important. The fate of the world depended on it.

"What about you?" Samantha asked Oren.

"He's helping," Kathy said.

"Right, but he's an oracle too." Samantha turned back to Oren. "Can't you use your abilities to find Vanita? I mean, not only are you blessed in the divine, but you're literally flesh-and-blood with this girl. Nobody here has a stronger connection than you."

"But he was just stabbed last night," Kathy said. "Isn't that too much stress?"

"It's not like I'm asking him to dance a jig!"

"I just think—"

"I'll do it," Oren said. "But I'm going to need a couple things."

The oracle relayed what he needed and the witches spent the next few minutes gathering them. The distraction felt like a step in the right direction and helped the sisters put their stress aside for a moment.

When they reconvened, Samantha walked around the room, burning the incense of hibiscus to make a more relaxing, inviting environment for divination.

At the coffee table, Kathy lit a purple candle, which represented astral magic, and a silver candle, which represented divination.

Oren, meanwhile, sat on the couch with his eyes closed. If it weren't for his lips murmuring slightly, the sisters would've thought he fell asleep.

Kathy waved the scent away from her nose. "Sam, I think that's enough. Put it away. Jeez!"

Samantha capped the thurible and set it on the coffee table beside the candles. She took a seat on the arm of the chair next to her sister. The two of them watched Oren, grateful that the pressure of finding Vanita was off of their shoulders for a moment. They didn't want to think about what they would do once they found her. So far, neither of them had come up with a good solution.

But one step at a time.

Oren looked peaceful, yet focused. He sat upright, seemingly oblivious to his injury or the smokey incense filling the room. The quiet words spilling from his mouth were foreign. Latin, perhaps. Ancient, for sure.

Finally, his eyes snapped open. "I know where she is."

"You do?" Kathy asked excitedly. "Where? Is she close by?"

"She's with Callum Ahmed," he said.

"Callum Almond?" Samantha asked.

"Ahmed," Oren corrected, then added, "He's a sorcerer."

CHAPTER 32

- JANUARY 1983 -

Vanita was determined not to answer her bedroom door when she heard someone knocking on the other side. She didn't want to talk to anyone, least of all her parents.

After several unanswered knocks, Oren walked in anyway.

"Hey," he said quietly, closing the door behind him.

Vanita looked up at him from her place on the window bench. She was picking at a thread from her jeans. "Hey."

He pulled up a chair and sat. "So I couldn't help but overhear what happened downstairs…"

"Did you know?"

Oren shrugged. "Not officially until today, but I'm not surprised. It's actually something I've been thinking about for a while. It never really made sense to me how much money we seemed to have. Divination consulting doesn't make you rich. And I know that we're not lavishly rich, but we're certainly well-off."

"If you had these suspicions then you should've told me," she snapped. *Was everyone in on this secret but me?* she wondered.

"I'm not the one you're really mad at," he said. "So don't take it out on me. If anything, you and I were on the same page. I didn't want to believe that this is how our parents made money, but it is what it is."

"*Our parents* have always made us seem so high and mighty because of our powers and how we need to be responsible with them." Vanita picked away more thread from the seam near her knee. "They've led us to believe that they're the examples we need to follow—and I did. Blindly. Stupidily."

"Vanny, just because they kept this secret from us—albeit, a huge secret—doesn't mean they're not still good people," Oren said. "If anything, it just goes to show how far they'll go to make sure you and I have a good life."

Vanita was shaking her head before he finished. She didn't want to give her parents any benefit. "If they wanted us to have a good life, they shouldn't have lied to us. Our life is a sham. Everything I thought was true isn't."

Oren rolled his eyes. "This doesn't change anything."

"It changes *everything*! If they lied about this, what else have they lied about? And how come we haven't seen the truth of their ways in all of our meditations and vision callings? Did they put a spell on us to block that insight? What other spells have they put on us? And if they've kept this secret, it obviously means that they don't trust us. Honestly, this lie makes me question if I can even trust them." She let out a heavy sigh and said in a quieter tone, "I just feel like a fraud for believing them."

"They're our parents. Of course we believed them. Why wouldn't we?"

"Exactly. They took advantage of that blind trust." She looked out the window. "At this point, I wish they weren't even my parents."

"You don't mean that," Oren said.

"Don't I? They've been *lying* to us, Oren. And they wouldn't have told us if I hadn't found out."

"You're upset, and I understand that, but don't discredit their love over this."

Vanita shook her head. She gave up on pulling out the thread from her jeans and smoothed it out. "It just makes me wonder, if our parents are frauds, do they really deserve to carry on the legacy of the amulet?"

CHAPTER 33

"I thought you killed Callum Ahmed?" Kathy blurted.

Oren nodded. "So did I. Stabbed him right in the heart. I watched him bleed out. How can he be alive?"

"Well, if he was powerful enough to build up your parents' trust and kill them, then I guess I could see how he could survive a knife wound," she said.

Samantha looked between the two of them, trying to keep up. "What are you two talking about?"

"Callum Ahmed is a bad man. Someone I thought I had already killed."

"But he's back, apparently," Kathy added.

"Yes, he is," Oren responded. "And apparently I never stopped him before like I had thought. Or maybe he was resurrected or something."

"Resurrection?" Kathy asked. "You think he got that power from someone?"

"Perhaps."

"Can someone tell me what the hell is going on?" Samantha shouted.

"Callum Ahmed is the sorcerer who killed my parents, which started the chain reactions that led me here today," Oren explained. "He's very powerful."

"As sorcerers are," Kathy added. "And hungry for power. No matter how much they have. If they gain enough, they might even be unstoppable."

"As he would be if he obtained possession of my family's amulet."

Samantha tucked her hair behind her ears and crossed her arms. "Let's rewind even further. I'm still caught up on the fact that—oh, I don't know—you're a *murderer*!"

"Not anymore than you are," Oren said. "You've killed magical beings before in an effort to stop them from spreading their demonic ways. What makes what you do right and what I did wrong?"

"He only killed to avenge his parents' death," Kathy said.

"And what about Vanita?" Samantha asked.

Oren shrugged. "Killing is never my goal. But if it comes to it and there is no other option, then yes, perhaps I would consider it."

"But she's your sister."

"And what if your sister betrayed you and threatened you and a whole host of other people?" he asked. "Innocent people?"

"We would never do that to each other," Samantha said.

"Stranger things have happened," Oren said.

Samantha avoided Kathy's eyes. She wasn't sure if he was implying her present situation or something hypothetical. Either way, she didn't want her certainty in Kathy's trust to be mistook for an apology.

Kathy was the first to change the subject. She turned to Oren and asked, "What did you see in the vision?"

"Vanita and Ahmed were at a party of some sort," he explained. "Formal. Elegant. Champagne, hors-d'oeuvres, a harpist playing softly in the conservatory. I assume that Ahmed has maintained his position at Gannon University. I recognized the residence."

"What does he do there?" Samantha asked, her arms still crossed. Her ears had perked up at the mention of her alma mater.

"Last I knew, he was a professor of history, as well as the department chair," Oren explained. "Of course, when I thought he had died, I thought that had ended. And I haven't been in Erie in some time to notice that he resurfaced."

"So Vanita was at the party with him?" Kathy asked.

Oren nodded. "Yes. It's clear that she's been working with him and the vision now proves it." He pushed at the cushions on the couch and struggled to his feet, cringing in pain at each movement. "I need to get to her."

Both sisters jumped to ease him back into his seat.

"You need to stay put," Samantha said. "You aren't going to do anyone any good if you bleed out and die on us. I didn't go through all of this to save you, just so you could die on my watch."

Kathy took a seat on the edge of the coffee table and patted his knee reassuringly. "See? Sam cares about you!"

He smirked. "Be that as it may, I have my family's honor to protect."

"Let us help," Kathy offered.

"Callum Ahmed is a sorcerer," Oren repeated. "He's probably filled my sister full of lies and promises of helping her once he claims possession of the amulet. None of it is true. Once he has what he wants, he will kill her. And the amulet could be lost from my family forever if he has possession of it."

"You think Vanita would just hand it over to him?" Samantha asked. "She didn't seem that stupid to me. I mean, she fooled us."

"It's not a chance I'm willing to take," he said.

Kathy looked over to her sister. "He's right. If Ahmed survived a knife wound to the heart, then he was already pretty powerful. And that was six years ago. Who knows how much power he's gained since then? And if he gets the amulet?" She shook her head.

"I know," Samantha said. "But how are we going to stop him?"

Kathy chewed on her lip, then turned to Oren. "You said you recognized where that party is?"

"From the looks of it, it was at the social house owned by the school," he said. "One of the city's original mansions."

"What about when?"

"Hmm." Oren thought. "Well, if the moon is to be believed, I would have to say it was a waning gibbous, much like the moon we're about to experience in the next few hours."

"So tonight?"

He nodded. "That would be my best guess."

"Good." Kathy made her way to the stairs.

"What was all of that about?" Samantha asked. "Where are you going?"

"Upstairs to find something to wear," she said. "I'm going to that party."

CHAPTER 34

This place looks swanky," Jeremy muttered to Kathy as they walked arm-in-arm down a brick walkway to the wide front porch.

"Hence the duds," she said.

They were both dressed to the nines. Kathy wore a blue gown that was snug around her body, but flowed down by her legs. It was strapless, which she regretted in the bitter cold, although she refused to wear a shawl or something for fear that it would ruin her outfit. After all, they needed to make an impression.

Jeremy was dressed in a black tuxedo, clearly pulled out of the back of his closet. Samantha had to take a lint roller to it to get all of the dust off the shoulders. Kathy didn't ask, but she suspected the last time he wore it was at his high school prom.

"Remember why we're here," Samantha told them. "And let *me* do the talking."

Her dress wasn't as flashy as Kathy's was, although it was still beautiful. Cherry red, with shoulder pads and a length that went to her ankles. Form fitting, but not tight. Simple, elegant, and practical.

"Right," Jeremy said. "We need to act like we belong. Otherwise they'll know we're just crashers."

Kathy didn't want to cancel on Jeremy for yet another night. That would doom their second chance at a relationship before it really got started. Besides, for the most part, this was just a party. They could dance, have fun, and enjoy the night, all while also searching for Vanita and Ahmed. Kathy had become a master at multitasking since she began taking college classes.

They reached the steps, but Samantha grabbed Kathy's arm and pulled her back.

"I can't believe you talked me into letting him come," she murmured quietly enough so Jeremy didn't hear.

"I told you," Kathy said. "We'll be more believable with dates." She wanted to add that Steven should've come, but she wasn't going to go there. The argument was too fresh and she still felt too guilty for being the reason it began.

Samantha studied her, likely thinking about Steven as well. Finally, she said, "You're *freezing*. You should've worn a sweater."

"And ruin the look?" Kathy asked with a grin. "I would never!"

The front door opened and a woman with hair-sprayed hair that nearly scraped the top of the doorframe stepped out. She had a pointy nose and squinty eyes. She wore a black top and white pants. Neither of them did any favors for her image. The outfit was probably something that cost a thousand dollars but looked like an art smock.

Jeremy stared at her and stammered, frozen in the face of even the slightest resistance.

Samantha marched up the steps and extended her hand to the woman. "Hi there! I'm Samantha and this is my sister, Kathy, and her boyfriend, Jeremy."

The woman loosely offered her hand. "I don't know you. You must have the wrong address."

"Oh no, we're a friend of your husband's," Samantha said. "Callum Ahmed?"

The woman furrowed her brow just the slightest. "Callum isn't married. I'm his housekeeper."

"Oh," Samantha scoffed with a forced laugh. "I should've known that!"

Kathy cringed. This was not going well. Why didn't she start using her persuasion power? That was the whole point of Samantha being the one to do the talking. It usually came so easy to her.

The woman stared at Samantha slack-jawed. "Are you

calling me frumpy? Do I look like the hired help? 'Oh, I'm *just* a housekeeper. No *wonder* I look a mess!'"

"No, that's not what I was saying!"

The woman rolled her eyes and stepped back to the door. "Please vacate the premises. I would most like to avoid calling the police."

With that, the front door closed and the three stood on the cold porch, avoiding each other's eyes for a moment.

"So much for that," Samantha finally said. She stepped back down the walkway. "I guess we'll have to come up with another plan."

Jeremy halfheartedly followed Samantha, but stopped when he saw Kathy hadn't moved. "Kath? What are you doing?"

Kathy shook her head. "No. I'm not going to quit. I'm getting us into that party."

"She already told us no," Samantha said.

"She told *you* no. Come on, Jeremy." Hooking her arm around her boyfriend, they stepped to the door again and knocked.

When the woman answered, she looked annoyed. "I thought I told you to leave. Please don't make a scene."

"I'm sorry about my sister," Kathy said. "She's just a fan of architecture and wanted to see the house from the inside and thought she'd tag along with me." She patted her chest. "I'm in Callum Ahmed's history class at Gannon. And this is my date. I believe we were invited to Callum's mid-semester party? You see, I misplaced my invitation. I think it must've slipped out of my bag at the library."

The woman regarded them skeptically, then looked past them at Samantha.

Kathy turned and glanced at Samantha, then back to the woman. "Oh, if my sister doesn't make the cut on the guest list, that's okay. I mean, she'll be upset, but she's also just trying to crash the party." She laughed nervously. "But would you mind if Jeremy and I came in? I mean, I would hate to miss the social event of the semester. What would I talk about in class?" She laughed again.

"What class are you taking?"

"History 101," Kathy offered, hoping beyond hope that it was a course he taught. After all, Samantha had made an assumption about Ahmed's marital status and got burned for it.

The faintest smile spread across the woman's lips. "I could tell you're a freshman. Yes, you two may enter. But not her."

Kathy turned and offered Samantha a guilty look. Her older sister looked betrayed and angry as she watched them enter. No matter what Kathy did, she seemed to be getting on Samantha's bad side today. Feelings aside, they needed to get into that party.

CHAPTER 35

After watching Kathy and Jeremy disappear into the party without her, Samantha stormed back to the car in her party dress. Oren waited in the passenger seat. His bleeding had stopped, although he was still visibly weak. The sisters had tried to get him to rest back at the house, but he insisted on staying. Besides, Samantha didn't want to further fuel the fire between her and Steven by asking him to keep an eye on Oren.

Once she was behind the wheel again, Samantha slammed the door shut. They were parked down the street a bit from the house. They had a perfect vantage point for staking it out. It helped that it was an old mansion, unobscured by the trees that had gone dormant for the winter.

"Where's Kathy?" Oren asked.

"Inside."

"And her boyfriend?"

"He's with her."

It had taken some delicate deceit to get both Jeremy and Oren in the car without Jeremy asking any questions. First, they had to put Oren in the car before Jeremy arrived so he wouldn't pick up on the fact that Oren had been stabbed. From there, it was simply explaining that Oren was a "friend" of Samantha's who would come along for the ride.

When they had arrived at the mansion and the trio got out to enter without Oren, he had explained away Jeremy's curiosities by saying that he was waiting to meet up with a friend at Gannon. Potentially, that ruse would be ruined depending on what happened inside.

Samantha just wished she could see what was going on. She slapped the steering wheel. "Ugh, why did I have to have a *mind* specialty? Why can't I have a forethought specialty, or whatever it is."

"Are you damning your powers?" Oren asked. "That seems unwise."

"No, I'm not—well, maybe I am," she said. "It's not like they've really been working for me lately anyway."

"In what way?"

She gestured toward the front door. "Like just now. I was pushing my persuasion power real hard. It was my first power! Something I've mastered since I was a teenager! But it didn't work on that lady."

"Perhaps she's immune."

Samantha gave Oren a side look. "Nobody's immune unless there's something funky going on. But that's not the only issue I've had with my power. I feel like I haven't heard as much chatter lately."

"Chatter?"

"I can read minds."

"Ah," Oren said. "A dangerous gift."

"I don't take advantage of it," she said. "I developed it about six months ago and at first I heard *everything*, regardless of whether I wanted to or not. Then I was able to cap it so I could only use the power when I intended. I was even starting to get good at it. But lately…I feel like I'm losing control. Of both my powers, actually."

"From what I've seen in my experiences, whenever inherent magic isn't working, it usually means that there's a stressor or something blocking the ability to come naturally."

"I know. I need to relax. But I don't see that happening anytime soon."

"Have you considered talking to someone about your stress?"

"Like a shrink?"

Oren shrugged. "Like a friend. Or your husband."

She waved off that suggestion. "Steven and I have been arguing a lot lately."

"I caught a glimpse of it earlier."

"Yeah, well, how am I supposed to react when I catch him in a lie?"

"Are you sure he was intentionally lying to you?"

"He kept the realtor a secret from me when we both agreed not to move anywhere!"

"That's not exactly what happened," Oren said. "Besides, did *he* agree not to move?"

Samantha nodded. "Yes, he did."

"Or did he agree to keep you happy at the expense of his own happiness?"

"That's not—he would've said something if he wasn't content with staying put. We've discussed it."

"Surprisingly, people don't often say what they really think," he said. "Clearly his actions show that he would like to move somewhere else. And while your sister was incorrect with her conclusion that your husband was having an affair, I think it could be a safe assessment that unless you both start *really* listening to each other and start picking up on the things that you're *not* saying, an affair on either part could be down the line for the two of you. The two of you don't want to create an environment where you can't be honest with each other."

Samantha let his words sink in as she watched the party. The night was getting darker and through the large windows, she could see people dancing and laughing inside. Despite the snow-covered, cold exterior, inside looked warm and inviting.

"I like being in control," Samantha said. "I like knowing what's going to happen next and how that's going to play out. I obviously know that life has curveballs. Being a witch has definitely shown me that. But for the most part, I like being in control of my future." She dropped her eyes down to her thumb working off the black paint from her fingernails. "Lately, though, things in my life have been happening in ways that seem out of my control."

"Such as?"

"Well, I'm a wife now," she said. "I knew that was going to be a big change, but I thought we'd generally still just be Samantha and Steven, just with a shared last name."

"Marriage is turning out to be different than you thought?"

"A bit, yeah," she said. "Not bad, I guess. Just…different. Like, I didn't think there'd be such a big *shift* in my mindset. I know we're essentially the same people we were before we got married, but in the back of my mind there's this voice that says, 'This is a lifelong commitment that you've made. There's no turning away from this now.'"

"That fear is typical in some of the newlyweds I've coached in the past. You just need to remember to persevere through it because you agreed to marry that person for a reason."

"I know. And I know it'll get better and I'll warm up to the idea, but it's just another layer. And then there's work, which I didn't think about when I planned my wedding. We got married right before the busiest part of the year for both of us at work, so now it seems like we barely see each other. And when we do, we argue."

"There's ups and downs of every part of life," Oren said. "You need to make it a priority to be nice to one another, even when it's difficult. Find a balance. Talk to each other."

"Yeah." Samantha sucked in her bottom lip, feeling the tears welling up in her eyes. "And then there's the biggest one of all." She paused, trying to wait for her emotions to settle enough so she could continue. "I've, uh, been having some health issues. Nothing deadly, I don't think. In fact, I think I might just be pregnant—or maybe could be. But it just brings up these old feelings about my mother."

"What happened with your mother?"

"She passed away when I was young." Samantha looked at him with tear-lined eyes. "I don't remember her much. And I honestly haven't been too terribly sad about her being gone because I've never really known what it's like to have a mother, so it's like I wasn't aware of all that she was missing. But now with the possibility that there might be something wrong with me, I'm afraid that I'm going to be like her and die before I've really had a chance to live. And arguing with Steven every day is not helping me feel like I'm making any progress. But instead of talking to each other, we just argue. Every damn day. I just…I feel like I'm being a bad wife."

Oren let her cry for a bit. She wiped away her tears, smudging her makeup. She glanced in the rearview mirror to clean herself up.

"Well," he finally said. "I know that I don't need the power of foresight to tell you that everything will work out as it's supposed to. What I can offer you in the meantime is some advice: hold your loved ones close. Your husband and your sister are your two greatest allies. Tell them what you're going through. Allow them to help carry the load from time-to-time. Be okay with not being in control."

She smirked through her tears. "But I *like* being in control."

He smiled back. "We both know that that's an unrealistic expectation."

"I know. I'll talk to Steven when I get home. Let's hope he's in the right mood to talk—"

"Regardless of his mood, you need to have a civilized conversation with him if you expect it to have any effect. *Take control* of your situation."

Samantha chuckled and sniffled, dabbing at her eyes again. "That's clever."

"It's true."

"I know. And I'll talk to him."

Although she felt better, the thought of exposing herself like that to Steven was scary. She had always been honest with him, but the thought of being so vulnerable with her insecurities that she didn't yet have solutions for was terrifying.

CHAPTER 36

We made it inside," Jeremy murmured to Kathy with delight. He struggled to stifle his smile, which brought one to Kathy's face. Even though she knew the true reason for their intrusion into the party, it still felt like they were just goofing off.

"Shh," she warned. "Let's not draw attention to ourselves."

Kathy led him into the conservatory, which overlooked the ornate garden in the yard. Even though it was snow-covered, the garden and the surrounding brick wall were adorned with lights that cast a glow even into the moody sunroom.

"Champagne?" Jeremy offered her a thin flute he must've snagged from a waiter on their journey to the sunroom.

"I would be delighted to indulge," she said, whimsy

flickering her tone of voice.

There was only one other couple in the conservatory, since the temperature was noticeably cooler in here. The large curtains framing the doorway were not just decorative, but practical too. The other couple looked out into the gardens, locked in a conversation about what the yard looked like in full bloom.

"Now," she said in a whisper, "if we're trying not going to get found out, we need to act like we belong."

"We need to talk to strangers?"

"Exactly," she said. "But we need to sound like we know what we're talking about and that we have connections. So you pull off your typical boyish charm and I'll see if I can scope out the guy who lives here."

"Why do you want to find him?" Jeremy asked. "Wouldn't that draw attention to us? The person who lives here must know that he didn't invite us to the party."

"Um…" Kathy hadn't thought about it from that perspective. She just needed to find Ahmed and Vanita so they could get the amulet back. "These rich guys know all kinds of people. And a professor? I already lied and said I was in his class. He probably doesn't know the names of even *half* of his students. Isn't that why professors have graduate assistants? To do the real work?"

Jeremy nodded. He had suffered through a class at Penn State Behrend that was very clearly taught by an inexperienced graduate student.

"So let's go back out there," she said, as if breaking a huddle.

"You find an approachable couple and I'll scan the crowd for the big guy. Maybe I can sweet talk us into a tour of the place and we can get an even better experience. Let's go!"

She stepped to break through the curtains back into the main parlor, but Jeremy pulled her back deeper into the shadows. Before she knew what was happening, he pinned her against the wall and kissed her. When he pulled away, she bit her bottom lip and smiled.

"What was that for?"

"This whole thing with getting dressed up, crashing a party, and sneaking around with you is, I don't know, kind of hot," he said.

She laughed at his admission. "Oh yeah? I'm glad you're getting turned on by the tux you've had in storage for the last five years."

"No, it's not that. Just…the experience. It's different than our usual thing. I like it."

She took his face in both her hands and kissed him on the lips. "I think it's fun too. But the fun is going to be very short-lived if we don't make ourselves public soon. I'm not about to be arrested for shacking up in the hall closet of a stranger's house."

He laughed. "Fine, fine. I'll relax."

Back out in the parlor, Jeremy approached an elderly couple, who seemed to be standing off by themselves. Kathy was at his side, but her eyes scanned the crowd in search of their magical targets.

"Gorgeous place," Jeremy said to the older gentleman. "Is this your first time here?"

The man nodded. "Yes, it's our first time. My wife has recently transferred to the history department after a long career in the English department."

"So you're a professor too?" Jeremy asked, perfectly playing the part.

The woman nodded. "I started at Gannon as a student in the forties. I stuck around until they started paying me!"

The couple and Jeremy all laughed. Kathy was too preoccupied. Her eyes were at the landing at the top of the stairs. She could see someone's back but couldn't tell if it was Ahmed or not.

Before they left, Oren had described Callum Ahmed as an esteemed man. Someone who thought very highly of himself. Perhaps most notable was the fact that he smoked a pipe and carried it around as an accessory to his person. According to Oren, the pipe also doubled as the sorcerer's wand.

Thanks to Oren's attempt to kill him all those years ago, Ahmed could be walking with a limp, or show some other indication that he struggled to breathe. After all, Oren had thought he was dead until just a few hours ago.

"I'm Richard Blumen," Jeremy lied easily. He extended his hand, first to the woman, who introduced herself as "Penelope Smithers," then to the man, who introduced himself as "Gregory Smithers."

"And this is my wife, Leslie." Jeremy reached over and touched Kathy's shoulder. Her attention snapped over the couple and she smiled widely.

"Hi! Nice to meet you both."

"Do you work in the history department as well?" Penelope asked. "I'm still learning new faces."

"No, I'm a student," Kathy said. She figured they should keep their lies consistent—Jeremy's name changes notwithstanding.

"Ah, I see," Penelope said, apparently losing interest.

"What are you studying?" Gregory asked. Clearly, it was only an effort to be polite.

Kathy's eyes wandered back up to the landing, hoping that the man in the burgundy suit would turn around. She thought it was Ahmed, but she couldn't be sure. Not until she saw his pipe—and perhaps Oren's amulet around his neck. She had a hunch that a power-hungry sorcerer wouldn't let something as strong as an ancient amulet go too far from his grasp.

"Leslie, honey," Jeremy pushed. He put his arm around her shoulder. "Mr. Smithers here would like to know what you're studying."

"Huh?" Kathy turned back to the conversation. "Oh, um…anthropology." She looked back up at the landing. The man in the burgundy suit was turning. If he had the pipe then she would—

"What an impressive field of study." Penelope lit up. "What

time period are you particularly interested in?"

The man in the suit turned and began to descend the stairs. Kathy didn't immediately notice anything in his hands. He descended, holding the banister with his right hand adorned with a gold ring on his finger that glinted in the light. He wore his shirt open-collared, revealing his graying chest hair beneath, but nothing else around his neck. As he came further down the curved stairs, he reached into his coat pocket and pulled something out—a pipe.

Kathy snatched Jeremy's hand. "I see someone we know, honey!"

"It was nice talking to you!" Jeremy called back to the Smithers as Kathy dragged him toward the base of the staircase.

Before Kathy could intercept Ahmed, though, she stumbled into Vanita, who looked very different than the last time Kathy saw her on the street.

Dressed in a flowing yellow gown, Vanita had cleaned up very nicely. She still had loads of jewelry and her hair was a bit messy, but she looked much more put together than she had only yesterday.

"Long time, no see," Vanita said to Kathy.

"Oh, who is this?" Jeremy asked.

Kathy ignored him and stared the oracle down. As she did, she noticed that something was missing. The amulet.

"Well, are you going to introduce me to this charming

young man?" Vanita eyed Jeremy with flirtatious eyes. "He is certainly…memorable."

"This is Jeremy," Kathy said with gritted teeth. "Jeremy, this is Vanita. She's…someone I know."

As she spoke, she watched as Ahmed joined the crowd in the parlor and disappeared into the dining room. If neither Vanita nor Ahmed had the amulet, that meant it was hidden somewhere in the house.

Vanita's hand lingered in Jeremy's when she introduced herself. "Such a firm grip. It's definitely something I could—"

The oracle stopped mid-sentence as Kathy froze the room. As much fun as she and Jeremy were having playing dress-up, she was here on a mission. And now that Vanita knew she was here, their fun time was over.

Kathy weaved around Vanita and stepped to the stairs. If the amulet was hidden anywhere, it would probably be up in one of the private rooms.

Hopefully she could find it before her magic lost its hold on the room and Vanita noticed she was gone.

CHAPTER 37

- FEBRUARY 1983 -

Vanita waited as the TA passed back the papers her history class had written. At the front of the lecture hall, Professor Callum Ahmed stood, critiquing the class's work.

He was a very well put together man. Always wearing a suit, sometimes of varying colors. The pipe he carried in his pocket and sometimes smoked during class was something that made him a bit of a legend around campus. It was a habit that was usually seen in older men—ones with graying hair and a loss of hearing.

Professor Ahmed was anything but that. He was certainly middle-aged, but had a certain quality about him that still made him attractive. Not that Vanita was interested in dating her professor, but even she had to admit that it would be hard to say no if he decided to take that route with her.

"None of these essays really wowed me," he said. "They were good—okay work—but nothing grabbed my attention and made me feel as though you fully understood the material. But, this is still the beginning of the semester so I went a little easy on the grades. Next time, however, I won't be. I expect to see better results."

The TA reached Vanita and handed hers back, which had a big red "C" on the front. Her jaw dropped, appalled. She had worked hard on that paper. Granted, the semester started right around the time she and her parents had stopped speaking to each other. Over the last month, she had cut off her family and moved out on her own—not an easy thing to do after she had been taken care of her entire life.

Still, she had put in a good, honest effort into this paper. And she had done her best to make a history paper engaging. There was only so much she could do with the source material: Japanese Feudalism.

"If there are any questions, I have about five minutes after class," Ahmed said. "But please, I am not willing to debate. If you have a question about a specific point in your paper, I would be happy to explain my reasoning, but these grades are final. Have a good day."

As everyone rose to leave, Vanita hauled her backpack over one shoulder and raced to the front.

"Um, Professor," she called to him. "I had a question about my grade."

"I will not discuss grades." He waved his hand, pushing her off.

"Well, it's just that I think that I did a great job of bringing the topic to life," she said. "Was there a particular point in my paper that you thought fell flat? Something I can improve on?"

Ahmed sighed, then reached for her paper. When he did, his fingers grazed hers and she was struck with a vision—the first one she had had in months.

Professor Ahmed walked down an empty corridor at Gannon University with a briefcase in his hand and his pipe hooked in the corner of his mouth. He walked with a purpose, a sense of urgency he tried to mask.

He climbed the stairwell and reached the landing halfway up, where a custodian was mopping the floor.

"Careful," the custodian warned, "the floor's wet. I haven't put the sign up yet."

Ahmed nodded and continued up the stairs. When he reached the top, he stopped and set his briefcase against the railing.

"Sir? Is there something I can help you with?" the custodian asked.

"Yes," Ahmed said. "Is your power limited to only nonmagical or can it manipulate the magical as well?"

The custodian's eyes widened in fear. He moved to race down the stairs, but Ahmed was too quick. Pulling his pipe out of his mouth, he waved it at the custodian, sending a streak of lightning at him. It struck the custodian, who convulsed and fell down the stairs to the bottom.

With his palm open, Ahmed waited for a magical light to shine toward him as he absorbed the man's powers. After the light faded, Ahmed replaced his pipe in his mouth, retrieved his briefcase, and continued down the hallway.

Vanita came out of the vision with a smirk.

"The problem with your paper," Ahmed said, "isn't the level of engagement. In fact, yours was one of the better written papers in class. The problem I had with your paper was the credibility. Where are your citations? How can I trust that the information you present is factual if I can't refer to any other articles or books to support your claims?"

She hadn't been listening. Her mind was spinning with a plan. More sinister than anything she had ever done. But it was justified, in her opinion.

"Vanita, are you listening?"

She snatched the paper out of his hand and tossed it aside. "I have a proposition for you."

CHAPTER 38

At the end of the hall, Kathy entered the room that was obviously Callum Ahmed's bedroom. Among the others that she had peeked in down the hall, this was by far the largest. In the center sat the large bed with ornate carvings into the oak wood frame. Above it, the coffered ceiling framed the bed, giving the room a more regal appearance.

As she stepped in further, Kathy noticed the wet bar and seating area in the corner, as well as a door that led to a private bathroom and walk-in closet.

Clearly, this part of the historic house had been updated.

Ignoring all of its lavishness, Kathy quickly turned to her task at hand: finding the amulet.

It was the second time today that she had tossed a room, so

she knew exactly where to start. She went straight to the walk-in closet and found the shelves that served as a dresser. The clothing was mostly formalwear, although the folded clothes were the typical T-shirts, underwear, and even a couple pairs of jeans. One-by-one, Kathy tossed them on the floor and listened for a heavy thud to indicate that something heavy had landed on the hardwood. Something that was hidden within the folds.

Nothing.

Turning her attention to the pull-out drawers beneath the shelves, she rifled through the jewelry. It was all men's wear—rings, watches, a golden chain necklace—but nothing resembled the amulet she saw around Oren's neck before Vanita stole it away.

Frustrated, Kathy stepped back into the bedroom. She could search the bedside tables or the bathroom, but she knew that she would probably come up empty. If Ahmed hadn't stashed it away in his own closet—somewhere deep within the confines of his private living quarters—then the likelihood of it being in a drawer beside his bed or laying on the vanity in the bathroom was slim.

No, Ahmed was smart. Which meant that he would hide it somewhere that wasn't so obvious. Somewhere that *wasn't* his bedroom.

Cracking open the door, Kathy peered out into the hallway to make sure the coast was clear. She could hear the murmured voices of the crowd below. Her magic had worn off, which meant that Vanita had noticed she was gone and would come looking for her soon. She didn't have much time.

Unfortunately, there were three other rooms off of the upstairs hallway, most of which led to bedrooms. Which one would Vanita and Ahmed hide the amulet in?

Desperate to find it, Kathy picked the door closest to the master bedroom and entered quietly. This room was smaller. Clearly, a guest bedroom. Yet it was just as stately. Moody lighting, art on the wall, and a similar ornate bed frame decorated the room. In the corner sat a dressing table, equipped with a plush seat and a mirror. On the table sat a lamp with a hand-sewn lampshade.

Most surprising of all the amenities in the room was the walk-in closet. It was smaller than the closet from the master, but it maintained much of the historic character that had been stripped from the largest bedroom. Original oak trim, darkened with age, and red and cream wallpaper lined the walls. The window overlooking the street indicated that the closet might've once been its own separate bedroom or nursery when the house was first built.

Ignoring the decorations, Kathy went straight for the jewelry drawers, as there were only a few garment bags hanging on the racks. Clearly, it was overflow clothing from the master closet.

There was more jewelry in these drawers. Women's pieces from bracelets to earrings to diamond rings to necklaces. Every drawer was filled with random pieces of jewelry, none of it organized nearly as well as it had been in the master. Still, in the second drawer, buried under a heap of costume jewelry, Kathy found the amulet.

As she lifted it in her hands, she could feel the power radiate from it and knew that the sorcerer would certainly be unable to resist its power. Yet somehow, Vanita had kept it away from him. Perhaps she's the one who hid it here.

With the amulet in hand, Kathy stepped back out into the bedroom and peeked out the door into the hallway. Coming up the top of the stairs was Jeremy and Vanita.

"Damn," Kathy swore under her breath. She ducked back in the bedroom and paced, trying to figure out what to do.

Kathy heard the doorknob turn just as she realized that if Vanita had been the one to hide the amulet, she would know which room to enter.

The witch made it back into the closet in time to close the door most of the way before her boyfriend and the oracle entered.

"I have a girlfriend," Jeremy said to Vanita in the other room.

"Sit down," Vanita said in a stern voice. "I know you weren't actually invited to this party."

Kathy looked around and tried to figure out what to do with the amulet. She didn't have a plan and she didn't know how the amulet worked, so she couldn't really use it herself. She didn't want to unleash its full power and blow away Jeremy in the process—or hurt anyone else downstairs.

ORACLE

With no pockets, Kathy slipped the amulet in the only other place she could think of—in her cleavage.

Let them try to get it from me there, she thought.

"Where is she?" Vanita asked Jeremy. "Where is that witch of a girlfriend you have?"

Shut up, shut up, shut up, Kathy thought. She didn't want Vanita to say too much and reveal her secret.

Turning to the window, Kathy looked out and could see Samantha's car. She was sitting in the front seat with Oren, looking toward the front door. Samantha wasn't even looking up in the tiny window. Kathy would need to draw more attention if she was going to signal to Samantha to come in and help her.

Unlatching the locks, Kathy quietly pushed the window open, hoping that it wouldn't creak with age.

"Who sent you? Was it Oren or the wit—where's that cold air coming from?" Vanita asked.

In the closet, Kathy cringed. She didn't account for the cold winter draft blowing in. She hung out the window and waved her arms. Samantha still wasn't paying attention and she knew that Vanita was about to walk in and find her.

"Sam! I need your help!" She managed to wave her arms in the air before Vanita stepped into the closet.

"There you are!" she said with a sneer. "And I see you've found something that belongs to me."

CHAPTER 39

Samantha shivered in her seat. The car was off, as a way to mask it among the other cars parked on the street. Being that it was late-February, the frigid air made that a questionable decision. As a way to distract herself from the cold, she decided to strike up a conversation with Oren.

"So how are you feeling?" she asked. "With your injuries?"

The oracle grunted as he shifted uncomfortably in his seat. "Well, I've been better."

"You need rest. You shouldn't be here."

He nodded. "I know. But I won't be able to until I know that the amulet is in good hands."

Samantha could sympathize with that. If the magic book had been stolen, she would be persistent to get it back. It was a family relic, just as the amulet was to Oren.

"Hopefully we'll hear something soon." She glanced back at the house, feeling anxious, worrying about what was going on inside without her. How Kathy was handling it and whether Jeremy was a help or hinderance.

"Hopefully," he said.

Samantha wished she could be inside with her sister. She wished she was back to one hundred percent. Maybe then Vanita never would've fooled her and Oren wouldn't have been stabbed.

"You know, if Kathy calls for help, there's no way you'll be able to make it into the house," she told him. "I mean, it took a while just to get you into the car. Not to mention the fact that you're not stitched up properly by a doctor, so who knows how easily those homemade stitches will tear open. You've already ruined our couch, I don't want you to ruin my car too."

"I know," he said. "And I hope it speaks volumes how much I'm trusting you and your sister to retrieve my family heirloom without me. I know I can trust you."

Samantha smiled at him. "Well, thanks for that. I promise, we'll—"

Oren pointed toward the house. "Is that your sister?"

She turned and looked, scanning the grounds before she spotted Kathy waving out of an upstairs window.

"Sam!" Kathy called. "I need your help!"

Samantha was reaching for the door just as Kathy turned

back to whatever she faced inside.

"Take note of the window," Oren told her. "So you don't waste time searching for the right room."

Forcing herself to stop, Samantha inspected the windows, noting that the one Kathy had been in was smaller. It was also the third in from the front of the house. That meant it was upstairs, to the side, toward the front.

"Got it," she said, then turned back to Oren. "You stay put."

Before waiting for an answer, Samantha slammed the car door and raced inside. This time, she was not going to be denied entry.

CHAPTER 40

Kathy looked down and saw that the amulet, snug in her chest, was glowing red. It was reacting to Vanita's presence.

It all made sense. It was a family amulet. Without someone in the family, the amulet's powers would be dormant. *That* was why Ahmed had kept Vanita around instead of insisting that she give it to him.

"Give me that!" Vanita tugged at the chain peeking out from the top of Kathy's dress and pulled the amulet out. "Now get out here and sit with lover boy!"

Kathy stepped into the room and took a seat beside Jeremy, who was visibly shaken. His eyes were wide and he stared at the floor, both knees bouncing with anxiety. His shoulders were tucked in and he laced his fingers together between his legs, trying to make himself as small and non-threatening as possible. He didn't even look up as Kathy took a seat beside him on the bed.

Vanita stood by the door and crossed her arms, watching them. Kathy was relieved that she didn't say anything that would give Jeremy any reason to suspect that Kathy was a witch. As it stood, right now he probably thought they were just getting robbed or about to be arrested for trespassing or something.

Moments later, the door opened and the smartly-dressed man Kathy had seen downstairs stepped in. He propped the pipe in the corner of his mouth and looked down at Kathy and Jeremy.

"So what do we have here?" he asked.

Jeremy's knees stopped shaking. He looked between the three of them. "What is this? Is this a joke? Are we—do you think we're someone else?"

Callum Ahmed looked at Jeremy with a funny look. He unbuttoned his suit jacket to put his hand on his hip. "I don't follow."

"You two are a couple, right?" He motioned between the sorcerer and the oracle. "So are we, but we're not—you know."

"Jeremy, *shut up*," Kathy hissed.

"I'm just trying to lay it all out before anyone gets their hopes up," he told her, then turned back to Ahmed and Vanita. "We're not...*swingers*."

"Swingers?" Ahmed said with a hint of a smile.

"Seriously, Jeremy, shut up," Kathy warned.

"Yeah, we just wanted to sneak into a fancy party and score some free drinks," he said. "I didn't think we'd be invited *upstairs.*"

Ahmed pointed his pipe at Jeremy and Kathy braced for impact, but nothing erupted from his magical outlet. Instead, the sorcerer turned to Vanita.

"This man has no idea what's truly going on, does he?" he asked with a laugh.

"It was this one who had this on her." Vanita held up the amulet for Ahmed, who reached for it but the oracle snatched it away. "Nuh-uh. Not so fast. You need me for this, remember?"

Jeremy leaned over to Kathy and whispered, "Crossdressers?"

Kathy elbowed him, but kept her eyes on Ahmed and Vanita.

"Fine then," Ahmed said to Vanita. "Have it your way. Use it on them." He motioned back to Kathy and Jeremy.

Vanita pointed to Kathy. "This one waved to someone outside. Her sister. We need to be prepared for additional company."

Leaning over again, Jeremy asked Kathy quietly, "Did Samantha stick around?"

"Quiet," Kathy said through clenched teeth.

"Her sister wouldn't launch an attack with all of these

people downstairs," Ahmed said. "What is her specialty?"

"The mind," Vanita said. "I'm not sure exactly how it manifests itself, but I wouldn't put it past her to strike if she thinks she can keep everyone else safe."

Ahmed stood up straighter. "Regardless. We need to be on the offensive and be ready in case this wit—"

The door came crashing in, slamming into Ahmed's back and sending him stumbling to the floor. On the other side, Samantha stood in her red dress and bare feet. Somewhere along the way, she had ditched her heels.

Vanita jumped to retaliate, grabbing ahold of the door and trying to shut Samantha out, but the witch was quicker. She delivered a powerful jab to Vanita's collar bone, then a quick swipe with her feet took out the oracle's feet and knocked her to the ground as well.

Kathy and Jeremy sprung to their feet. Kathy knew she should freeze the room, but as long as Vanita held firm to the amulet, it would be impossible to remove it from her grip. The magical entity would cling to the closest it could find to its rightful owner. Kathy nor Samantha would be able to successfully pull it away from her grip while frozen.

On his knees, Ahmed delivered a hard punch into Samantha's thigh, causing her to cry out and land hard on the ground. He looked to the floor and lunged for his pipe as Jeremy stepped forward.

"Don't you hit a woman like that!" He stepped with

purpose, only stopping as Kathy hooked her arm with his and pulled him back.

"Jeremy, relax," she said. "Samantha can take care of herself."

"He hit her!"

"I know, but you have no idea what you're up against."

During the struggle, both Vanita and Ahmed had recovered and were now on their feet. Ahmed held his pipe out, ready to unleash his magic while Vanita gripped the amulet in her fist, the gem glowing red.

"Now," Ahmed said with a heavy breath. "Let's try this again."

CHAPTER 41

Vanita paced the floor in front of Samantha, Kathy, and Jeremy, who were all squished together on the bed. Callum Ahmed leaned against the wall, puffing on his pipe.

"So you refuse to tell me where Oren is?" Vanita asked the group.

Both sisters remained tight-lipped, stubborn until the very end. Samantha knew how much Oren trusted her and Kathy with the amulet and they were letting him down. The least they could do was not rat him out and hopefully buy some time so they could get the amulet back safely in his hands.

"I have a right to know where my brother is." She leaned down close to Jeremy and grabbed his chin in her hand.

"You're cute, but unfortunately I highly doubt you have the information I desire."

"You have the amulet," Ahmed said. "Use it to find your brother yourself so you can take rightful ownership of the stupid thing and have full power after we kill him."

"Kill him!" Jeremy blurted in surprise.

Kathy shushed him.

"Well, I suppose I can give it a try," Vanita said. "I've never used it before, although it *does* belong to my family. How hard can it be to figure out?"

At the dressing table in the corner, she took a seat and closed her eyes, her fist tight around the amulet.

Samantha tried to measure whether they would be successful in any attempt to get to the door, but Ahmed stood over them like a prison guard ready to strike. Besides, if they couldn't get out without the amulet, escaping wouldn't matter because they'd be dead soon anyway.

Just as Vanita was doing, the sisters needed to rely on their powers. Trouble was, Samantha didn't have the faith in hers anymore until she could figure out why nothing worked the way she expected it to. The incident downstairs when she first tried to enter the party scarred her.

Worse, she knew that Kathy couldn't freeze the room because Vanita was clutching the amulet so tightly. And if she was in the process of using something so powerful, no amount of witch magic would be able to break that connection. It'd be a miracle if Kathy's power would even *work* on Vanita while she wielded the amulet.

"I see him," Vanita declared with a smile.

"You do?" Ahmed asked, excitedly. "Where is he?"

Her eyes flashed open in a bright red glow.

"What the—?" Jeremy murmured, but everyone ignored him.

"He's nearby," Vanita said.

Ahmed stepped closer. "Yes, where?"

"He's right—"

The door crashed open, again slamming into Ahmed. Oren rushed in, one hand holding the wound on his side, where the faintest trickle of blood had already started to bleed through his clothes. His face was contorted in pain, but still he pressed on.

Samantha didn't hesitate. She jumped to her feet and rushed to Vanita, wrestling with her for the amulet. Behind her, she could hear Kathy assisting Oren with Ahmed, likely playing keep-away with his pipe.

Vanita pushed at Samantha, going right for her face, but Samantha twisted her body around, letting the amulet's chain dig into Vanita's flesh. Soon, the oracle shouted out and released her hold on the gem, which Samantha tried to pull toward her quickly.

At the last second, Vanita tightened her grip and held tight on the chain.

"Let it go," she said. "It's rightfully mine."

"No, it's rightfully Oren's," Samantha corrected. "You're going to abuse it."

"And who says that?" Vanita pulled tighter on the chain. "How is it fair that he gets it simply because he's the oldest? Or is it because he's a man? When do I, a woman, get to maintain my family's power?"

"This isn't some sexist debate." Samantha could feel the metal digging into her fingers. "Look what this has already driven you to do! You *stabbed* your brother for it!"

"Because it's *mine*!"

"No!" Ahmed shouted, just as Samantha heard a crunch behind her.

At the same time, the chain finally gave way and broke, sending both Samantha and Vanita falling back. Samantha held tight to the amulet and hurried to her feet, where Ahmed was already stepping toward her.

"Give it to me," he demanded with his hand out toward Samantha. "I need something to direct my power."

Just beyond Ahmed, Samantha saw Jeremy's dumbfounded expression as he sat helpless on the bed taking it all in. This was the most he had seen in all his time with Kathy.

Picking up on the stunned look on his face, Kathy waved her hand at her boyfriend, who froze in place. Ahmed and Vanita both noticed the use of Kathy's power and Samantha took that opportunity to toss the amulet to Oren, who caught it with the hand that wasn't clutching his side.

Ahmed pushed Samantha out of the way and she crashed into the door but remained on her feet. He charged at Oren, but the oracle held up the amulet and kept the sorcerer at bay.

The amulet glowed brightly. Oren's eyes shone red, as did the stab wound in his side, which quickly stitched itself up and healed completely.

The amulet was finally with its rightful keeper.

"Finally!" Vanita cried out. "You have it! Thank the gods!"

"Why are you happy?" Kathy asked.

"Brother, you can save me from this torment," Vanita said. Tears pooled in her eyes. "This man—this *sorcerer*—coerced me into using the amulet for harmful gains."

"What are you saying?" Samantha asked. "That this is all a ruse orchestrated by Ahmed?"

"It's a lie!" Ahmed shouted. "You came to me and asked me to kill your family so that you could take ownership of the amulet! You convinced me the two of us could work as a team! That was before I realized your complete incompetence."

Oren shook his head, his eyes still glowing red. "I can see the truth, Vanita. What this man says is true. You're the one who asked him to kill us all. *You're* the reason our mother and father are dead!"

Vanita continued to cry. "Oren, please, no, you have to believe me!"

"Save the tears," he said. "I know they're fake."

Immediately, she dropped the act and wiped the few

droplets that had fallen on her cheeks. "You never fell for any sob stories."

"You killed them with no remorse," Oren went on. "I need to have the same objectivity in your demise."

Genuine shock spread across Vanita's face. "No, Oren! You wouldn't do that! You wouldn't kill your own sister!"

Oren raised the amulet above his head. It shone a bright red as its power coursed through Oren's body. With the hand that was once holding his side, Oren extended it out toward Ahmed, sending a powerful stream of light at the sorcerer. Within seconds, Callum Ahmed was reduced to dust on the hardwood floor.

"Oren, you need to think clearly," Vanita said. "I'm the only family you have left. There's no one other than me. We need to stick up for each other! Protect each other. We're all we have left!"

"My sister died when she hired someone to kill our parents," he said, turning his attention to her.

"So you're going to kill me?" she asked. "If what I did was so terrible, how does that make you any better? If you say I'm a murderer, then so are you!"

Oren ignored her and took a step forward. Another flash of light erupted from the amulet and struck Vanita. Samantha watched in amazement, wondering if she had misjudged Oren's ability to handle the amulet. Perhaps they should've come up with a way to destroy it instead.

When the light receded, Vanita remained, although she collapsed to the floor unconscious. The light disappeared from around Oren and he slumped down, reaching for the wall to catch himself.

"What did you do?" Kathy asked nervously. She was afraid to help him.

Oren's shoulders shook as he wept.

"What is it?" Samantha asked. "Is she…?"

"I used the amulet to purify the intentions in the room," he explained.

"Which means, what, exactly?" Kathy asked.

"For Ahmed, that meant his demise. For Vanita, it meant stripping her of her powers…and her memory."

"Her memory of what?" Samantha knew just how complicated the mind was. If her powers would cooperate, it was something she wanted to continue to explore.

"Of the amulet," he said. "Of our power. Of our family."

The sisters exchanged looks. Samantha didn't think that there existed magic strong enough to completely erase memories of someone's own family. Then again, she didn't think they'd ever faced anything as powerful as the amulet Oren still clutched in his hand.

"Through Vanita's selfishness and greed," Oren said, "I not only lost my parents, but my only sister as well. I have no more family."

CHAPTER 42

Samantha still couldn't believe the news when she walked through the door the next day after work. It was late. The sun had set. And although she hadn't originally wanted to go to her appointment *after* work, the late hour was the last thing on her mind.

As she pulled off her gloves, scarf, and coat at the door, she noted that Steven and Kathy were sitting at opposite sides of the dining room table, both working. Kathy, likely on a paper for her class, and Steven probably on accounts he brought home from work.

Was there an apology I missed? Samantha wondered.

Immediately, she dismissed the thought. The way they both kept their head down, even as Samantha entered, told her that nothing had changed. Only their need for space to work. Besides, she could feel the tension radiating off of both of them.

Kathy broke the silence first when she looked up at her sister. "What's the matter?"

Samantha didn't even deny that something was bothering her. She knew it was obvious. "I just got back from the doctor."

Steven scoffed. "You know, I should've gone with you. I offered to!"

"I didn't think it was anything at all."

"But…?" Kathy pushed.

"The blood work showed it," Samantha said, ignoring Kathy. "And now all the symptoms make sense. The passing out, feeling sick, being tired, moody—it's all normal."

"Normal for *what*?" Steven asked, a hint of annoyance in his voice.

"I'm pregnant," she admitted with a smile.

Kathy's jaw dropped, even as her cheeks turned up into a smile. She threw her hands in the air and shot to her feet, racing to hug her sister. Steven got to his feet and came around to do the same.

Samantha braced herself for the impact of both Kathy and Steven wrapping her in a hug, smiles on all of their faces.

"Oh my gosh, Sam!" Kathy squealed. "I'm so happy for you! For you both! You're going to be a mommy—oh, and I'm going to be an aunt!"

Samantha beamed. "Aunt Kathy. That has a nice ring to it."

"So there's nothing wrong with you?" Steven asked as they pulled away. "It's just symptoms of the pregnancy?"

"Exactly. I didn't think passing out was part of it, but apparently it's more common than you'd think," Samantha explained. "My doctor said that it happens with low blood pressure from hormones."

"Hormones like adrenaline?" Kathy asked. "We definitely have enough of that pumping through our veins."

Samantha shrugged. "I'm sure that doesn't help."

"But there's nothing wrong?" Steven asked. "With you or the baby?"

She shook her head. "The doctor doesn't think so. I have a sonogram scheduled for next month, so we'll find out then."

Steven kissed his wife, then pressed his forehead against hers. "I am so happy."

"You don't think it's too soon?" she asked. "We just got married."

"Too soon? Honey, now we have a reason for that extra bedroom upstairs! And the tree in the backyard would be perfect for a swing—a baby one at first, of course, but we can upgrade to a regular one when he or she gets bigger."

Samantha smiled. Not only because Steven was clearly very excited about the baby, but also because his desire to move had obviously faded. He must've been telling the truth about that realtor. She made a mental note to officially apologize to him when they were alone.

"Congratulations, you guys!" Kathy pulled Samantha in for another hug. She turned and faced Steven. They both hesitated, then broke into a smile and hugged each other. "You're both going to make great parents."

"Thanks," Steven said.

"Do you mind if I tell Jeremy? I'm hoping this will pull him out of the daze he's been in since I had Oren erase certain parts of his memory of last night."

"No, go ahead," Samantha said. "But make sure to emphasize that it's still really early. A lot can happen!"

"Everything will be fine, Sam!" Kathy promised. "Stop worrying!" She hurried off into the kitchen to the phone.

Alone, Samantha turned to Steven. "Are you really happy about this?"

He took her hands. "Absolutely. Aren't you?"

She took a deep breath, then smiled. "I am. But…I'm also scared."

He nodded. "It's a lot of unknown we're heading into."

Samantha thought about her mother and wished that she were still alive to help her through this. Even though she hadn't developed a deep connection to her mother, she still mourned the fact that she would never have this experience with her. Or her father, for that matter, but that was a different circumstance.

"Yeah, it is," Samantha admitted.

She thought of her conversation with Oren the night before. How she needed to let people help her carry the weight she was carrying. How she needed to be more open and honest, especially with Steven. If there was ever a time to try it, this was it.

"I'm already stressed out," she said. "Between work and being a witch and trying to maintain all of my relationships…it's a lot."

"I've noticed."

"And now the pregnancy is just another layer to all of that and I'm going to need your help with more than I'd care to admit," she said. "This isn't easy for me, asking for help."

"I know. But let's think about it. Your workload will subside. Tax season will come and go. Figuring out how we work as husband and wife will get easier. And you've always managed being a witch before. You'll figure it out. I promise I'll try to be more open to that part of your life."

She took another deep breath and pulled him close to her. Feeling his arms around her helped center her world, which had seemed like it was spinning lately. "Thanks for that. It means a lot."

"I just want you to be happy. And I know it's going to be hard for both of us, especially you. But I also know that you can handle it all. And I'll be there for you the whole time."

"Promise?"

He pulled away and put a hand on her stomach. "Promise. After all, we're going to be a family."

A carnival birthday party for a one-year-old turns terrifying when a little girl lets out a scream from within the funhouse. Samantha and Kathy rush in to rescue her, only to find a demented clown hovering over the girl, feasting on her screams. He gets away, leaving the sisters scratching their heads as to who or what it might be.

After asking around, the staff all claim that there are no clowns employed by the carnival, which doesn't explain what the girls witnessed. To make matters worse, Kathy is pulled away after her friend has a surprising revelation about her boyfriend, Jeremy. That leaves Samantha, whose powers haven't been working exactly right ever since she became pregnant.

As the sisters struggle to find answers, another kid is found unconscious deep inside the funhouse tent. With hundreds of children arriving at the carnival for fun and games, the clock is ticking for the sisters to find a way to stop what lurks inside. And its only a matter of time before he gets what he's after.

Trickster is the eighth book in the Coven series, which serves as a prequel to the Under the Moon series.

TRICKSTER

COVEN: BOOK 8

Read on for an excerpt of the next book in
the Coven series!

DAVID NETH

CHAPTER 1

~ MAY 1989 ~

Samantha felt the tears well up in her eyes. Her breath shuddered and her chest heaved.

This was her worst nightmare.

"So you've been lying to me?" Steven asked at the foot of the stairs.

"I was trying to make you feel included." She stood in the foyer, her meager attempt to keep him from leaving.

"By keeping a secret from me?" He turned and started up the stairs.

She raced after him and tugged on his arm. The two of them stopped halfway up the stairs. "I didn't want you to feel alone or left out because you were the only one who wasn't a witch."

"Look around, Sam! I'm the only man in this house too and

somehow I manage!" He pulled his hand away from hers and continued up the stairs. "You should've been honest with me."

"I didn't want you to have to worry about our child having magic and being in danger. I didn't want to put that pressure on you, like you have with me." She followed him right into their bedroom.

Steven pulled open the closet and dug out the suitcase from the back. "But I still would be worried once they came. You just didn't want me to know about it. It'd be like you keeping the whole pregnancy from me. It's *purposely* deceitful and I just can't see past that."

"I wasn't trying to deceive you." She looked down at the suitcase open on the bed. Then, as Steven opened his dresser and started tossing his clothes in, she asked in a panicked voice, "What are you doing? Why are you packing?"

"I'm leaving, Samantha."

She came around the bed, getting between him and the suitcase. "No! We can talk about this! I'm sorry! I'm so sorry!" Tears ran down her cheeks as her voice grew more hysterical.

"It's a little too late for that, Sam." He stepped around her and dumped another drawer of clothes in the suitcase. He wasn't stopping to fold or sort anything. Clearly, he wanted to get out of there as soon as possible. "If you lied about this, how do I know you're not lying about something else? Or will again when the kid actually comes?"

"Please." Her voice strained and she felt her knees go weak.

She clutched on to him, another desperate attempt to change the outcome. "Please don't go. This was all a mistake. I didn't mean for this—I didn't think you'd be this hurt by this!"

"Well, then, you shouldn't have lied."

She clung to his arm, trying to hug him, but also trying to stop him from packing. If he would just look at her, maybe then he would agree to stay. "Let's just take a moment to cool down. Talk about this later after we've had some time to think. Steven, I love you."

For the first time, he met her eyes. What she saw wasn't love or compassion. It was pain, mixed with anger and, if she was being honest with herself, a hint of disgust.

She found herself repulsive. How could she do this to him? To their marriage?

"I need to go." He zipped his suitcase, which surprisingly he didn't have any trouble closing up. Using two hands, he took ahold of the handles and hauled it to the door and down the stairs.

Samantha was on his tail, following behind. "Can you at least give me the number of where you're staying? Maybe we can talk tonight after a little bit."

"I don't know where I'm going, exactly. I just know I need to go." He stood by the front door and fished for his keys on the table.

Samantha spotted them first and reached for them, clutching them to her chest so he couldn't leave.

"Give me my keys, Sam."

"No," she said firmly. "You're not going. This isn't—let's talk. We can fix this!"

"No, we can't. There's nothing to talk about. You made the decision for me when you lied about our child. And now you continue to try to control me by keeping me here. This is it. This is the final straw. We're done."

Samantha let out a sob and felt her knees weaken at his words. "No!"

Steven held out his hand, the other on his suitcase. His face was stoic. She searched it for any regret. Any pain. Any sense of loss that their marriage was over.

Nothing.

Slowly, she gave in and handed him his keys. He walked through the front door without a goodbye. She stood on the porch and watched as he wheeled the suitcase to his car, tossed it in the trunk, then drove off.

CHAPTER 2

- TWO DAYS BEFORE -

The brakes hissed on the train as it came to its stopping point at Erie Forge and Steel. Alex Trillanski approached one of the cars and pulled open the sliding metal door, a cigarette hanging out of his mouth.

He'd been smoking a lot more lately. Nearly two packs a day. He'd never been under this much stress before. He wasn't sleeping, his meals were usually interrupted, and he knew from his doctor that he wasn't drinking nearly enough water. The smoking didn't help his health, but it sure did help him relax.

Hopping up into the cargo car, Alex began passing crates out the door to his coworkers, who lined up to pile them on the trucks and carry them inside. George, who started at F&S the same year as Alex, jumped up in the car with him to move the cargo out faster. The quicker they could get the train unloaded, the quicker they could get started on their work, and the quicker they could go home.

"How's your boy doing?" George asked as Alex passed another crate to someone outside the train. "Still getting over that bug?"

"Last night was terrible. Up every hour. Puking his guts out. You know how many loads of laundry I did during the hours when a man's supposed to be sleeping? Jeez, if I wasn't switching the sheets, I was getting him a glass of water, or trying to rock him back to sleep. I just hope I haven't caught it from him." He flicked the ashes from the tip of his cigarette, then stuck it back in the corner of his mouth to reach for another crate.

"Feeling any tickle in your throat?"

"Not yet, but I'll tell ya, if I keep having my sleep interrupted like this, it won't be long before I'm out too."

"Is the missus still working nights?"

Alex grunted as he lifted a particularly heavy crate. "Damn right. And after the shit she deals with over at the prison, she deserves a break too."

Irene was a security guard at the county prison. She had signed up for nights thinking that it would be perfect so she and Alex didn't have to pay for child care. Someone would always be home. Too bad the wonky schedules were kicking their butts.

"I'll bet," George said. "Wouldn't want that job, no matter how much they're paying."

"She's making decent money," Alex admitted. "But we have that credit card debt still."

"Those things'll do ya in."

Alex took a final drag of his cigarette and then flicked the butt out the door into the stone near the tracks. He looked around the train car. It was mostly empty. The remaining crates were marked for another location. Except the one in the corner. That had no labels on it.

"You know what the deal is with this one?" he asked George.

"Not sure. Probably not even ours."

Alex stepped forward to inspect the metal crate closer. "There's some weird markings on it. Looks almost…satanic or some shit."

George approached, wiping the sweat from his brow with the sleeve of his shirt. "Probably just graffiti from some kids who snuck on the train at night. Let's open it up, see if we can't figure out where it's going."

Unlike the wooden crates that had been pinned shut with thin metal staples, this crate had its own lever system to lock the doors. Alex grabbed the handle and tried to twist it open. It wouldn't budge at first and he grunted with the effort.

George grabbed ahold of another prong on the lever and helped. With the two of them, they managed to loosen it enough so that it spun freely.

"Damn, that was tight," Alex muttered.

George snickered behind him, but stopped when his

coworker pulled the door open and a large plume of black smoke erupted in their faces, sending both men falling backward on their butts in the train car.

"What the hell was that!" George gasped as the black cloud flew out of the train car and disappeared into the early morning sky.

"No idea," Alex muttered. He looked over at George. "You okay, man?"

George didn't answer. His eyes were locked on the inside of the metal crate. Slowly, he raised his hand, which was shaking with fear, and pointed inside.

Alex peered around the door of the crate and his jaw dropped.

The crate was completely empty. The only sign that it had once contained something were the deep scratches all over the metal inside. Whatever they had released was not something to be messed with.

CHAPTER 3

This one is cute!" Kathy held up a pink flowing top that she had picked from the clothing rack.

Samantha made a face. "How often do you see me wearing pink?"

"Well, you're going to be a mom. Possibly to a little girl. A lot of pink might be in your near future."

"That doesn't mean I need to get a jump start on it," Samantha said. "Besides, I'm looking for maternity *pants*. Preferably something that doesn't make me *look* pregnant."

Samantha was only three months pregnant and yet her growing belly was already making it difficult to fit into her pants. She feared what her body might look like at the end of the pregnancy. Last week, Kathy suggested that there might be twins but Samantha's stone cold glare shut that idea down real fast. Besides, her last sonogram confirmed that there was only one baby. He or she just happened to be demanding a lot of Samantha's body. Luckily, though, she had't experienced any morning sickness so far. She hoped it stayed that way. That didn't mean she hadn't been nauseated nearly every day. She just hadn't gotten sick from it.

"You're going to have to embrace it sometime." Kathy sifted through another rack of clothes. "You're only going to get bigger."

"I know, but in the meantime, I need something cute to wear to Laurel's party tomorrow." Samantha browsed through the next rack over. "Something that looks good and that I feel good in."

"Keep in mind, the party tomorrow is for her daughter, who is only a year old," Kathy said. "To be honest, I think the whole special preview day of the carnival is a bit over-the-top."

Laurel was one of Samantha's friends from high school, who also knew Kathy. After high school, Laurel met her husband, Charles, during her first year of college. He and his family lived in a large home on one of the tree-lined streets off of South Shore Drive, near Frontier Park. After Laurel had dropped out of college to get married, Samantha wondered whether Laurel had married for love or wealth.

Regardless, Laurel was now a mother to a beautiful one-year-old daughter named Ashley. And thanks to the deep pockets of her husband's family, Ashley was going to get a huge birthday bash that likely cost loads of money. Never mind the fact that Ashley probably wouldn't ever remember it.

"Well, that's Laurel's style now," Samantha said. "But it'll be fun. Even if we're the only two kid-less people there."

"Technically, *I'm* the only one without a kid," Kathy said. "Yours is just still cooking."

Samantha laughed and rubbed her belly. "Don't remind me."

"Can we talk about how weird a carnival party is for a one-year-old?" Kathy draped a pair of pants over her arm that she thought Samantha might like. "Is it for the kid or is it to show off in front of the neighbors?"

"The carnival was going to be in town anyway," Samantha explained. "Laurel just paid for a private preview a day early for her party."

"I'm sure that cost a pretty penny."

Shrugging, Samantha moved on to another rack. "I'm still debating whether I want to announce my pregnancy tomorrow. It all depends on what I'm wearing."

"I thought since you were past the first trimester and have a lower chance of miscarrying that you were more confident in the pregnancy?" Kathy came beside her sister and pushed away a pair of pants she was considering. "Not those—you're going to be a mother, not a grandmother."

Ignoring her sister's jab, Samantha walked over to the shoe

department and sat on a bench. Immediately, she felt relief in her feet, which had swollen after a day of shopping. "I am, but I'm still not sure. I don't want to steal Ashley's thunder."

"She's only a year old and her mother got her a carnival for her birthday. She's going to be overshadowed *just* a smidge."

Samantha shrugged her agreement.

"Besides, I'm just happy that it's been three months since we've had any sort of magical crisis."

"Knock on wood!" Samantha waved her finger at her sister. "Every time we assume that, something always comes up. I would like to make it through my pregnancy and the first six months of my child's life without having to chase down any bad guys."

"First of all, that year-and-a-half stretch is *seriously* wishful thinking. Something's bound to come up. Even so, I think we're safe for this weekend. I mean, what's going to happen at a baby's birthday party? Is a clown going to jump out and scare us? Doesn't exactly sound like something we'd need to take care of."

Samantha shook her head. "Stranger things have happened."

FIND ALL THE BOOKS IN THE COVEN SERIES!

More by the Author

To find more books by the author, visit
DavidNethBooks.com/Books

* * *

Subscribe to his newsletter to be the first to know of new
releases and special deals!
DavidNethBooks.com/Newsletter

* * *

**If you enjoyed the book, please consider leaving a
review on Goodreads or the retailer you bought it from.**
Reviews help potential readers determine whether
they'll enjoy a book, so any comments on what you
thought of the story would be very helpful!

About the Author

David Neth is the author of the Coven series, the Under the Moon series, Heat series, the Fuse series, and other stories. He lives in Batavia, NY, where he dreams of a successful publishing career and opening his own bookstore.

Also writes small town romance as D. Allen.

www.DavidNethBooks.com

www.facebook.com/DavidNethBooks